C000072475

DESTINY

RISING

Space Colony Journals - Vol 2

Gail Daley

KINDLE ASIN:
 E-book ISBN
D2D Print Book ISBN 9781393218692

Dedication

To the readers of my books who give me the inspiration to keep writing, and to my husband and son who never gave up on me.

About This Book

A marriage of convenience between two determined, strong willed people sparks a planetary war and puts at risk everyone they love.

Laird Genevieve O'Teague, beautiful, and strong-willed became leader of her people at seventeen. Colonel Gideon Michaels had been a soldier who controlled thousands of fighters in the war. When it was over he needed a new home for his orphan niece and his adopted son. Genevieve's offer would provide both, but could he follow his heart and learn to trust and love his new wife? Vensoog is under attack by pirates and when Genevieve and his niece are kidnapped by an agent of the Thieves Guild, Genevieve and Gideon must learn to rely on each other and their newfound love to defeat their enemies.

The Space Colony Journals are an epic tale of a family's struggle to survive. Meet the courageous women and dangerous men who carve a home on the alien world of Vensoog.

Contents

Acknowledgmen ts

I would like to thank my Beta Readers, Betsy and Ron McDermott and my son Andrew S. Daley who took busy time out of their schedules to read this book and help me tighten it up.

Past Imperfect

GENEVIEVE, Laird of the O'Teague Clan, stood on the terrace of her room in the original O'Teague Manor and looked towards the spaceport. It couldn't be seen from here yet she knew it was there and felt its presence like a lead weight on her heart. She grimaced. Today was her last day as an unmarried woman. Tomorrow, the ship Dancing Gryphon would begin unloading its passengers and cargo. Her younger sister Katherine would be bringing down the man who was going to be sharing her life and her bed for the next year. Although she knew and accepted the necessity for the coming Handfasting, she had hidden her inner reluctance from Katherine, whose plan it had been, and from her clan who were depending on her for leadership.

When the Karamine biogenetic weapon struck Vensoog in the final three years of the war killing or sterilizing all the male humans, it had been a devastating blow to the two-hundred-year-old colony. Since the Karaminetes only used the bio-bomb on planets they planned to resettle, the virus had a very short life span and soon dissipated.

Two years later, the treaty declaring peace was signed and the Confederated Worlds began the slow road to recovery. It did not take the Vensoog Clans long to realize they were in deep trouble. The additional loss of most of the men and woman on the five ships supplied to the war effort by the Vensoog Clans had only worsened the problem created by the bioweapon. With no additional children being born, the colony population would die out within three to four generations.

Genevieve's younger sister Katherine had come up with a solution to the dilemma. The planet needed a fresh supply of healthy sperm to maintain a good genetic balance. Since the Vensoog people shunned the cloning of humans, Katherine had concluded they needed a fresh batch of male colonists. Vensoog had been lucky in that they still had a viable planetary ecosystem; a few planets had simply been burned off, leaving thousands of souls homeless. Since the weapon seemed to have had a very short shelf life, bringing in a fresh supply of genetic material should solve the problem. In accordance with Katherine's plan, she and her Aunt Corrine had gone to Fenris, where most of the returning soldiers from this area were being decommissioned and offered them a new home, providing they were willing to join one of the Vensoog Clans by entering a 'Year And A Day' Handfasting rite with a suitable Vensoog woman. Or if the new immigrant didn't want to be matched for some reason they could choose to supply sperm or ova (if the soldier happened to be female) for the planetary genetic banks. These Donations would be later developed into embryos and implanted in living volunteers. Tomorrow Katherine and representatives from the other Clans would be returning home with the first round of new immigrants.

To persuade their fellow clanswomen to participate, both Katherine and Genevieve had signed up to be Handfasted. Showing the strength of their confidence and belief in the program by signing up for it inspired the young women of the Clan to participate. Katherine's Handfasting program, unlike the previous Match program used by the Makers was designed to pair couples not just for genetic diversity, but the personality and lifestyles of the women with their prospective husbands, thus ensuring a happy joining. The couples would be joined for a Year And A Day, after which they could dissolve the union or opt for the 'Forever And A Day' Handfasting Ceremony, which was a lifetime commitment. Not all the new immigrants were male, some of the returning soldiers had been women and they too were offered Clan membership. Those immigrants already in committed relationships had been offered full clan membership for their families as well, but they were expected to Donate to the planetary banks. The sperm or ova would later be combined, as the Maker Program deemed suitable to create children. The donors could raise the children if they chose, but the most common situation was for the children to be adopted by childless clan members.

Genevieve had a great deal of faith in her sister's programming skills, but she knew the kind of bad boy traits she had been attracted to in the past would not make a suitable husband in the long run, and probably not in the short term either. To rule wisely, she needed the kind of man who would prove a good counterbalance for her. She needed and wanted the kind of partnership she had seen in her parents before their deaths. She didn't need another handsome, selfish charmer in her life. Don't be such a wuss she chastised herself. This man won't be like Gregor. You're older and wiser now and Katherine's program would have taken into account what she needed wouldn't it? Genevieve studied the image of Gideon Michaels on her personal com. He certainly didn't look like a man who depended on his charm or looks to get by. He wasn't bad looking, but his blunt features held both strength and determination. His face showed none of the wild recklessness that had characterized Gregor Ivanov.

Maybe it would be all right, she thought hopefully. She needed a good, solid man who would come to care for the Clan as much as she did she reminded herself, and going by the steady set of Gideon's eyes and the firm set of his mouth under that beak of a nose, Katherine had provided that. Genevieve knew that many of the Clan thought she still mourned the loss of the wild young man from the neighboring clan who had so nearly charmed her into marriage. Well, what they didn't know couldn't hurt them, she thought wryly.

The scent of the river and the soft breeze of the cooling summer night caused eleven years to drop away and she was again that seventeen-year-old girl facing the man she might have loved and refusing to elope with him and abandon her people and Vensoog to the mercies of the Karamites. It had been a shock to realize Gregor didn't care what happened to her or Clan O'Teague if he wasn't going to rule. She had stared at him in disbelief and horror when she recognized that he had fully intended to take over the Clan when they married, regulating her to an insignificant nothing. Gregor had apparently intended to use her status as Laird of O'Teague as a steppingstone to conquer the rest of Vensoog and overthrow the current Matriarchal Clan system. When the war disrupted his plans, he had decided to run rather than stay and defend Vensoog from the Karamines.

At the beginning of the war, the Parliamentary Council had announced that as a member of the Confederated Worlds, Vensoog was requested to supply both resources and staffing for five troop ships, which they had done. Genevieve's father had commanded one of them. The Blackhand, Gregor's ship in orbit, was not on the list of ships provided by Vensoog. In fact,

Genevieve had begun to suspect that the Blackhands crew was responsible for the recent raiding of outlying O'Teague farms. What's more, she had discovered that Gregor knew something about the raids he wasn't sharing with his Grand Duke, but she had no proof of anything and she had been reluctant to admit she could have been so wrong about him. When Gregor had come back tonight to ask her to escape with him on the Blackhand, he told her that as first officer he could guarantee her a place aboard ship. She had refused and in the end, she had used her special *talent* against him to keep him from forcing her to go with him. When he realized she meant what she said, he had damned her as he went to join the crew of the shuttle waiting for him. As a final insult, he had shot into her airsled, trapping her ten miles from the nearest homestead and preventing her from warning anyone about the coming raid.

Her youngest sister Drusilla burst in abruptly jerking her thoughts back to the present.

"Aren't you getting ready yet? We have that banquet in Port Recovery tonight with the other Clan chiefs and we need to leave in about an hour."

Genevieve smiled at her. Drusilla was turning into a lovely young woman. Drusilla had very ably taken over the management of O'Teague lands while Genevieve had been attending Katherine's seat in

Parliament. She had organized tomorrow's ceremony and the journey back to Glass Isle. Much tinier than Genevieve, she still had the family red hair and grey eyes.

"I'll be ready when it's time. I was just thinking," Genevieve replied. "Is that what you're planning to wear?"

"Why not? I'm just the youngest sister, I don't have to intimidate or impress anyone tonight," Drusilla replied. At sixteen, her fresh face was bare of makeup, and she had yet to put her short dark red hair into the elaborate hairstyles favored by the elite of the Clans.

"Oh no, you don't," retorted her sister. "It's time you took your place among us as a woman of power. You planned and organized all of this.

You should take credit for it. Come on, I think I have a gown that will become you and Mary will dress your hair."

As the sisters dressed, Genevieve reminded Drusilla she needed to speak privately to LaDoña DeMedici so she could pass on the message Katherine had sent.

"Do you think she will listen?" asked Drusilla doubtfully. "Isn't it kind of a criticism of Doña Sabina? I mean we'll be sort of implying she can't handle the job, aren't we?"

Genevieve smiled at her approvingly. "That's a very astute observation. For that reason, I intend to speak to her alone and be as tactful as I can. I intend to hand her the crystal Katherine sent and urge her to listen to it in private. I want everyone to have eyes on you and not notice when I do it."

Once dressed, the two sisters stood in front of the mirror in Genevieve's dressing room examining their appearance. For Drusilla's first public appearance as an adult, Genevieve had put her into brilliant white with a dragon silk, off the shoulder blouse and dressed her dark red hair with small white flowers. The fitted girdle cupping her full breasts was white as were the loose pants and filmy knee-length skirt split up each side to her hips. The only touches of color were the opalescent pendant of the Dragon Talkers, which she was entitled to wear, and a pair of red quartz drop earrings. Drusilla most certainly didn't look like a child tonight. Her

Quirka, Toula who accompanied her everywhere, had been provided with a jeweled collar in matching stones.

Genevieve herself had dressed in her favorite dark green in the same style, and she had wound her fiery red hair into a neat chignon held in place by the golden diadem of her office as Laird. She had been amused when Gorla, her own Quirka had insisted on picking through her jewelry box for a suitable bracelet to wear as a collar.

Seeing the stunned look on her baby sister's face when she caught her first glimpse of her mirrored image, Genevieve chuckled. "You aren't a little girl anymore so get used to it, sweetie. Next Planting Festival the Makers will be giving you your Match List and I predict you'll need to beat the young men off with a stick. I know there isn't much to choose from right now, but we will be getting some new families joining the clan this time as well as Katherine's soldiers; perhaps there will be some young men your age. Even if there are no one you like in this round of immigrants, there might be someone in the next wave. This won't be the last group of displaced colonists to take advantage of our offer you know. Katherine left the program running on Fenris." She frowned, thinking she still had to choose a suitable clanswoman to administer the program on Fenris as well as the other three planets where displaced refugees were being kept.

"Are you nervous Genevieve? I

mean about meeting—ah—Gideon, wasn't it?" Drusilla asked.

Genevieve's smile turned wry. "Yes, I am, I suppose. I have a lot of faith in Katherine's programming skills, but you may not remember that I don't have a very good track record in choosing men."

Drusilla glanced at her speculatively, "That wasn't your fault. I know what he did."

"I knew what he was doing too," her sister said grimly. "I just couldn't seem to break free of him until the last, and I had help to do that, didn't I?"

Drusilla looked a little self-conscious. "You would have done it on your own eventually. You were fighting it."

"Yes, but maybe not before he

managed to drag me aboard that ship."

"That wasn't going to happen," Drusilla said firmly.

"Well, it's in the past. Better to forget it and move on," Genevieve agreed.

The next day, Genevieve and Drusilla waited in the arrival dome in Port Recovery for the first set of the new colonists to arrive. Because she had wanted a look at Lewiston, Genevieve had arranged for them to be there in time to see the DeMedici party arrive.

"He looks like a vid hero," Drusilla whispered to her as they watched him escort Doña Sabina through the doors.

"Yes," Genevieve replied dryly, "all flash and no substance." Just as

Gregor had proved to be, she added mentally. If Katherine's information about Lewiston's plans was correct though he might prove a much more formidable opponent that Gregor ever was. While they waited, she continued to watch him out of the corner of her eye to see if she could learn more of his intentions.

Their small party watched the first wave of the DeMedici's leave the dome and the Yang's arrive. Lewiston and Doña Sabina however, stayed around, obviously waiting on something.

"They look like tough customers," Drusilla remarked to her after seeing the contingent of men, women and families arriving with Nü-Huang Toshi Ishimara.

"Well, they are soldiers,"

Genevieve retorted, "not really surprising they'd look like it. I'm glad Toshi Ishimara recruited families the way we did. Did you happen to notice that there weren't any children with Lewiston's group?"

"I wonder, is that because Doña Sabina refused to bring them or because Lewiston didn't want them?"

"I doubt if she would have refused. It's more likely Lewiston thought families would be a liability to his plans."

About a half hour later, Katherine and Zack walked through the doors with the first party of their new clan members.

Genevieve was only a second behind Drusilla in swamping their sister in a welcoming hug.

"We made it," Katherine declared unnecessarily.

"So I see," Genevieve retorted. "How was the trip out?"

Katherine made a face. "Space sick as usual for the first three days but it's gone now." She gestured a tall bronze-skinned woman holding two toddlers forward. "Jayne, this is my sister Genevieve, your new Laird. Genevieve this is Jayne, who has agreed to take over as governess for my new family."

Genevieve nodded graciously. "Welcome to Vensoog, Mistress Jayne. I hope you and your children will be happy here."

"Thank you, ma'am," the woman replied.

While Katherine was introducing Jayne to the kennel mistress Margie and her new nanny dogs, Genevieve had time to take stock of the men who had followed Katherine off the shuttle. She was uncomfortably aware of Gideon Michaels studying her as well. She was about to take matters into her own hands and introduce herself when Katherine turned back to her.

"Genevieve, may I present Colonel Gideon Michaels, his son Lucas and his niece Jayla?"

Genevieve held out her hand and Gideon bowed over it, brushing it with a kiss. "Lady Genevieve, I am honored to meet you," he said, retaining his grip on her hand when he rose.

She smiled back at him. "Just Genevieve, please. Since we are to be Handfasted, I suggest we start

with first names instead of titles."
She turned to Lucas and Jayla.
"These are your wards?"

"Yes, this is Lucas Llewelyn and
Jayla Michaels." He kicked Lucas in
the ankle to get his attention since
the boy had apparently not heard
the introduction; he had been
staring dumbstruck at Drusilla ever
since he'd seen her.

"What? Oh, pleased to meet you
ma'am," Lucas said, bowing, but his
eyes went straight back to Drusilla.

Seeing what had drawn his gaze,
Genevieve's lips twitched, but she
turned her attention to Jayla.
"Welcome to Vensoog, Lady Jayla,"
she said as the girl, having been
coached by Katherine on the trip
out, dropped a curtsey. "Lord Lucas,
I am pleased to meet you. I can see

you will be a welcome addition to the Clan."

She gestured Drusilla forward. "Gideon, this is my youngest sister, Lady Drusilla. Drusilla has been largely responsible for organizing the ceremony this afternoon and the journey back to Glass City we will take later this week."

"Pleased to meet you," Drusilla said shyly, blushing when she met Lucas' openly admiring eyes.

"Excuse me," Genevieve murmured to Gideon, gently freeing her hand. "Protocol," as she moved back over to Katherine.

"Lady Genevieve, Lady Drusilla," Katherine said formally. "This is my fiancée Zackery Jackson," she said gesturing to the dark, wiry man standing next to her, "and his wards, the Ladies Violet and Lucinda, and his nephews Lord Rupert and Lord Roderick. And this," she added going to stand behind a young redheaded girl with sharp green eyes, and putting her hands on both the girl's shoulders, "is my First Daughter, Lady Juliette O'Teague 'Ni Jones. Everyone, this is my sister, your new Laird, the Lady Genevieve O'Teague, and my younger sister Lady Drusilla."

Genevieve's eyebrows rose in surprise because somehow in all the communications Katherine hadn't yet informed her that she had chosen a First. She held out both hands to Juliette and said, "Welcome to our family, First Daughter. I am so pleased to meet all of you."

Katherine nodded her thanks. "If

you will come with me M'Lady, I'll present you to some of the other families who landed with us. We can do the formal presentation after everyone has arrived at the Manor house."

"Didn't Aunt Corrine come down with you?" asked Drusilla.

"Corrine and Vernal will come down with the last group. I hope you don't mind, Genevieve, but I invited Captain Heidelberg and his officers to the wedding feast this afternoon, so I hope they will accompany the last landing party," Katherine added.

Largely thanks to Drusilla's organization and Katherine's efficiency, the first group of new O'Teague clansmen went aboard the paddleboat Saucy Salsa, and headed down the channel towards the outer islands less than an hour after they arrived.

Genevieve had been absurdly conscious of Gideon's presence while she performed her duties as hostess. Finally, to her relief the family was settled in chairs on the deck as the boat made its ponderous way through the traffic. Gorla, her Quirka, had inspected Gideon earlier from Genevieve's shoulder and seemed to accept him.

"She's a cute little thing," he remarked as Gorla preened visibly under his regard.

"Yes, and vain too, I'm afraid. Behave yourself, Gorla!" she scolded. "I'm sorry, I didn't have much time to make you welcome earlier."

A deep rumble of masculine laughter answered her. "Not to worry," he said. "I'm just enjoying the sights. It's been a long time since I had leisure just to look around and not worry about where the next attack was going to come from."

"You were career military?" Genevieve asked.

"Yes I was, but now I have Lucas and Jayla to care for. I was ready for something different after the war in any case."

"Well, I can't promise you no more fighting as we do have the occasional raid from the Wilders in the hills and from a few from Outlaw space ships, but on the whole, we're a pretty peaceful bunch," Genevieve said.

Gideon nodded. "I understand from Katherine, that handling those types of incursions will be my primary responsibility?" he asked.

"Yes. Traditionally, the Laird's spouse does handle security for both the Clan and in Glass Harbor City," Genevieve responded. "If you are comfortable with the duty, in the O'Teague Clan the Laird's husband also coordinates Planetary Security, that of Port Recovery and the waterways used for travel with his opposites in the other Clans."

"At least I won't be bored," he said smiling.

"It kept my father pretty busy," she acknowledged. "I don't know what types of things interest you yet though but if you want to take on other pursuits, there will be time for them."

"Perhaps there are some things we can do together?" he asked, reaching for her hand again.

Genevieve put hers into it, enjoying the feel of strength carefully controlled as he clasped hers. "I'm sure we can find something. We will have to return to Port Recovery in a couple of weeks though. There is a Security Council meeting scheduled for six weeks from now. By then all the Clans should have been able to assimilate their new members and we can introduce our new Heads of Security to each other. I probably should warn you that this year it is our clan's responsibility to chair the meeting of the Security Council."

"Always?" he asked curiously.

"No, just for this year. The Security Chair position rotates every year. When we first settled here, a rotating schedule was set up so no one clan would be able to establish dominance over the others. The Founders were very concerned about not giving any Clan an excuse to set up a power monopoly. Usually we don't have so many new members to introduce in a session, but so many of the ten Security Council members went off to war that this time we probably will have at least six new members. I thought if I went with you it would give us some time without the entire clan watching us."

"Did you say ten members?" he asked curiously. "I thought there were only eight clans."

"There are, but the Talker's Guild has a member and so do the Independent Fishers."

Gideon nodded approvingly. "How long will it take for us to travel back and forth?"

"We have air sleds available which make Port Recovery only about a day's travel from home. We'll use one of them," she said. "I think we should spend the time until the meeting traveling around the Clan territories so you can get to know those of us who didn't come to meet you," she added.

He nodded in agreement. "Thank you for arranging some time for us to get to know each other out of the limelight, Genevieve. Seeing the territory is a good idea too. It will give me some idea of what defenses are available and what areas would be likely targets of any Jacks. To design a proper defense against an attack, I really need to see the topography of the area."

"Jacks?" she asked curiously.

He shrugged. "In the forces, we nicknamed the planetary raiders Jacks because they so often ah—hijacked items that didn't belong to them."

She grinned at him. "Was that a joke?"

He grinned back at her. "Well, it is a bad pun, I admit, but that's what we called them."

She felt herself relax as their mutual laugher broke some of the tension she had been feeling. It was nice to realize her new husband had a sense of humor matching her own.

Bless Katherine's programming, she thought. "Well," she continued, "after we return from the meeting, we still won't be totally tied to the Clan territory. We will be returning to Port Recovery each quarter when the Security Council meets. We will be returning for the Planting and Harvest Solstice Celebrations. Those are mainly social functions. Traditionally all the young men and women who have come of age are given a Match List of genetically suitable mates and the celebration provides a time and a place for them to meet young people from other clans. Attending the festivals helps me to keep up with who is who and who is doing what in the other clans."

He nodded in agreement. "It

should help me keep up with things."

"Your Lucas seemed really taken with my little sister," Genevieve remarked, changing the subject. She was watching the two of them leaning over the rail as Drusilla pointed out a family of Water Dragons feeding in the shallows on the shore.

"I did notice that," Gideon agreed. " I would have said he was struck dumb when he saw her. I'm afraid he hasn't had much experience around girls his age outside of those in the military academy. I was fortunate to get him a placement there while I was serving, but since he was due to graduate this year, he elected to come with me when I decided to emigrate."

"Well, Drusilla hasn't had much experience with young men her age either," Genevieve remarked. "We lost so many from the fever when the bio-bomb hit us. I reminded her just this week, that next Planting she would be getting her Match List from the Makers—"

"The Makers? What or who is that? You mentioned Match Lists earlier, but I didn't really understand what it meant," Gideon said.

"The Makers oversee the genetic tracking program that keeps our colony gene pool healthy," Genevieve replied. "Every year during the Planting and Harvest Festivals, all men and women who are of age are given a Match List of acceptable breeding partners."

"Ah—Breeding partners?" he asked incredously.

"Well, the Makers don't put it that crudely, but that is what it amounts to. The two Festivals are traditionally the time when the eligible candidates from all the clans gather in Port Recovery City. The social aspects ensure the mixing of the population and the lists help to prevent inbreeding within a clan. A lot of myths and misinformation about the Maker program are widely held and many engagements are arranged for couples who meet during Planting and Harvest Festivals simply because of the widespread acceptance that your list has your ideal match somewhere on it."

Hearing the irony in her voice, he

looked at her sharply. "Not true?" he inquired.

Genevieve made a face. "I suppose that is a matter of opinion. I found it to be not true at all when I got my list. And when Katherine was reworking the program to take to Fenris, I learned the Maker program was designed to ensure genetic diversity. It barely gives lip service to the emotional harmony of the couples involved. To give equal weight to each partner's needs, social status and personal likes and dislikes, Katherine had to re-write that part of the program completely. In my opinion, That misbegotten program has probably created more unhappy marriages than happy ones," she snorted.

"As I understand it then, you

were given such a list the year you turned seventeen?" Gideon pursued, obviously interested in her reasoning. "Do I take it you didn't like the results?"

"Well, let's just say I caught one of the men on my list raiding O'Teague land right before the war was declared," Genevieve replied grimly. "Gregor was from the Ivanov Clan across the channel and anytime he was caught in O'Teague territory, he used the excuse that he was there to court me to be where he wasn't supposed to be. And he—well let's just say that I found him to be less than honorable in his treatment of women. Before she left for Fenris I asked Katherine to ensure that her changes were implemented into the Maker program that will be used from now on."

Gideon looked thoughtful. "They just let you do that?"

"I didn't ask permission," Genevieve told him.

Overhearing this last, Zack attempted to turn a laugh into a cough, gave up and howled. Gideon stared at him, puzzled. "What is so funny?"

Still laughing, Zack replied, "Not asking permission for stuff like that must run in the family. Remind me to tell you a story about how I ended up with so many nephews and cousins living on Fenris sometime. I bet your Makers won't notice any changes to the program either—Katherine's good."

Genevieve had seen the outdoor pavilion and other preparations

Drusilla had arranged for the arrival and Handfasting ceremony for the new couples, but she felt she was seeing it through new eyes when she showed it to Gideon. Several smaller colorful dome roofs had been fastened together to form a larger area for the Handfasting ceremony and wedding feast. The cupolas were held up with poles wrapped in colorful ribbons. To take advantage of the breeze coming in off the water, no sidewalls had been put up so the entire area was open to the beach. Decorated tables of food with stasis shielding were already laid out for the afternoon and evening meals. Folding chairs had been placed around other tables set up for dining. A leaf-covered arbor for the Handfasting ceremonies itself had been erected off to the side. Behind and a little to the right of the arbor were two smaller tables holding a stack of red and silver braided ribbons, glasses and clear decanters filled with a golden syrup.

Up the hill from the pavilion were a series of larger connected domes enfolding the main house and dormitories. Extensive and fragrant gardens marked with stone paths led up from the rotunda toward the main house. Twenty or thirty smaller, colorful porta domes had been set up to provide privacy for the newlywed couples at secluded spots in the gardens as well. Behind the flower gardens were the acres of fruit trees and a large vegetable garden that supplied the manor with food.

One of the acolytes struck a crystal gong and a single clear note pealed. Everyone quieted, directing their eyes towards the tiny woman who would be officiating at the Handfasting ceremony. She stood under a canopy of green, sunlight filtering down through the leaves. The woman was wearing what Gideon had learned was traditional dress for women on Vensoog, a loose blouse with a vest laced in under her breasts, soft pants and a knee-length split skirt in rainbow shades. The colors made her eyes seem an even more vivid green than the arbor. Her white hair was braided in a coronet around her face. A large multi-colored crystal pendant rested on her breast, and large drops of the same stones were braided into her hair and hung from her ears; she was attended by two slim teenagers similarly dressed but in paler tones.

"Good afternoon," her voice had a deep bell-like quality. "For those who do not know me, I am High Priestess Arella of Clan O'Teague. I will be performing the Handfasting ceremonies today. Since we have quite a few couples to unite this afternoon, each ritual will be brief. I will ask each couple to come forward and join me under the Greenleaf, we will perform the service, and then you will be free to enjoy the arranged festivities until it is time for the brides to leave for the wedding bower. If there are any here who wish for the Forever and A

Day Handfasting, please let me know when you come forward." Arella consulted the infopad next to her.

"Genevieve and Gideon, please join me."

When the Laird and her betrothed had joined her, Arella said, "Please turn and face one another. Each of you cross your arms and take the others hands."

She picked up a thin, braided red and silver cord and laid it over their wrists, allowing the ends to dangle.

"Genevieve, Gideon, your crossed arms and joined hands create the symbol for Infinity. Today, we ask that the Light Of The Divine shine upon this union for a year and a day. In that spirit, I offer a blessing to this Handfasting."

"Blessed be this Handfasting with the offerings from the East — new beginnings that come each day with the dawn, junction of the heart, soul, body and mind."

"Blessed be this Handfasting with the offerings of the South — the untroubled heart, the heat of passion, and the tenderness of a loving home."

"Blessed be this Handfasting with the offerings of the West — the hastening eagerness of a raging river, the softness and pure cleansing of a rainstorm, and faithfulness as deep as the ocean."

"Blessed be this Handfasting with the offerings of the North — a solid footing on which to build your lives, richness and growth of your home, and the strength to be found by embracing one another at the end of the day."

Arella wrapped the dangling ends of the cord around the wrists of the bride and groom, binding them together loosely and tying a knot.

"The bonds of this Handfasting are not formed by these ribbons, or even by the knots connecting them. They are formed instead by your vows, by your pledge, to love and honor each other for a year and a day, at which time these vows may be renewed or dissolved by each according to their lights. Genevieve, Gideon, do you agree with the terms of this Handfasting?"

"We agree," they said in unison, and then Genevieve and Gideon stepped forward, hands still clasped, and kissed. Arella touched the cord and it slid off their hands, still tied. The acolyte a slim teenager in a pale robe stepped forward with a tray holding one of the glass boxes. Arella placed the cord inside the box and gestured for Gideon and Genevieve to each hold opposite ends of the box. The acolyte stepped back returning the tray to the table, where the second acolyte placed another empty box on it.

"By blood this oath is taken, on this day and in this hour," Arella intoned, touching the box with a small gold wand. Everyone felt the small surge of power. He had been warned to expect it so Gideon held firmly onto his end when the sharp stab of pain in his palm caused a drop of blood to form on his end of the box. Blood from a similar prick on Genevieve's hand met his in the center. The edges disappeared as the box sealed and their names and the date scrolled across the top in red. Examining his hand later, he found only a small pink scar had formed on his palm.

"This Knot is a symbol of your union. Hold it fast and give it an honored place in your home."

Genevieve slipped the box into a pocket of her wedding dress and Arella gestured the acolyte to step forward again, this time holding a tray with a clear decanter and two glasses. "For love and fertility," Arella said, pouring a small amount of golden syrup into the glasses. The two spouts of the decanter enabled both glasses to be filled at once with the same amount of liquid.

Genevieve and Gideon each held the glass to the other's lips as they drank, and then set the glasses back on the tray for the acolyte to take back to the table.

"Thank you Arella." Genevieve motioned for Lucas and Jayla to come forward. Holding Gideon's hand, she stepped up beside them.

"The O'Teague presents her new family, my husband Lord Gideon *ni'*Warlord of Clan O'Teague, his son Lucas and niece Jayla." She made the announcement and led the way from the arbor to make room for the next couple.

Jayla looked at her. "Why didn't you say I was your First Daughter, the way Katherine did with Juliette when she introduced her to you," she demanded.

Genevieve took a deep breath. She would have much preferred not to have this conversation at this time. "I didn't announce it, because it isn't true," she said mildly. "The position of First Daughter is not one that is automatically given by birth or family position. It isn't just a title either; it requires a lot of hard work and dedication. You and I don't know each other well enough for either of us to make the decision if you will be cut out for the duties, or even if you want it once you understand the responsibility. I hope that we can become friends as we get to know one another. Perhaps this decision can be brought up later when we know more about each other."

"You don't like me," Jayla

declared, a hint of tears in her voice as well as anger.

"Jayla—" Gideon began in annoyance just as Genevieve spoke.

"That isn't true," Genevieve said quietly. "I just don't know you. I hope we will get to like each other very much—"

Jayla dashed tears from her eyes and said stiffly, "May I be excused? I'm tired. I would like to go take a nap."

"Of course, dear," Genevieve said calmly, "As soon as dinner is over. You wouldn't want the other girls to think you are upset about anything, and they will if you leave so early."

Gideon had opened his mouth again but closed it at a slight shake of Genevieve's head. They watched Jayla as she stalked off to the table where Zacks children were sitting.

"I beg your pardon," he said, frustrated. "That was out of line. She just isn't happy and I don't know what to do about it."

Genevieve found herself patting his arm in reassurance. "It's alright. I expect these last few months have been a lot for her to handle. Didn't she lose her parents just a few months before you pulled her out of school? Her whole life has been turned upside down. Her parents are gone and so are her friends from school, she has a new father and a new home with new customs. It's actually reassuring she feels safe enough with you to lash out a little."

He gave her an odd look. "You're very understanding," he said.

"I lost my parents at a young age

too and I remember what that was like," she said. "Oh, I was not as young as Jayla, but a lot of responsibility got dropped on me before I felt I was ready. When mother died in childbirth, suddenly I was Laird with the entire weight of the Clan riding on every decision I made. Unlike Jayla, I didn't have anyone it was safe to lash out at, but I sure wanted to. Give her time. I'm sure she'll regain her balance eventually."

"I hope so," Gideon returned, looking thoughtful. He didn't say so, but his memories of his late sister-in-law Celia, made him doubt Jayla would feel any need to change her behavior. He loved his brother's daughter, but he found her attitude frustrating. Genevieve's responses to things like Jayla's behavior had caught him by surprise several times since meeting her. The Vensoog ladies certainly seemed to have gotten different training, perhaps, he thought hopefully, they would be able to pass some of that onto Jayla.

When Zack and Katherine had returned to their table to watch the rest of the ceremonies, Gideon took the opportunity to ask Zack what had been in the syrup they drank during the ceremony.

Zack shrugged. "Payome, I think Katherine called it. She tells me it's traditional during the ceremony. It's supposed to make the first night a little easier. Apparently, it's a mild aphrodisiac with a touch of soother. She says the effects usually last a couple of hours so it won't wear off before the couple goes to bed." He grinned, "Since Katherine and I are pretty well at ease with each other, I don't think we're going to need it— Vernal and Corrine either, but you might," he teased Gideon, who snorted and cuffed him affectionately on the shoulder.

Corrine and Vernal chose to become handfasted, opting for the more involved Forever and A Day ceremony. Several couples of the same sex chose to announce their Handfasting at that time as well. As expected, the individual Handfasting ceremonies had taken most of the afternoon and part of the evening, and then any new single members were presented to the Clan.

The wedding feast turned into quite a party. Genevieve and Gideon as hosts presided over the head table attended by Katherine and Zack and Corrine and Vernal. As special witnesses, the Captain and his officers from the Dancing Gryphon had been seated with them. Drusilla had a place there as well, but she was seldom to be found sitting down. She kept jumping up to attend to many small problems that seemed require her attention. She had provided music so the couples could dance with each other as well as games for the children.

To Genevieve's silent amusement, Lucas seemed to have been designated as Drusilla's dinner partner instead of sitting with the other children. It's started already she thought. I'm going to need a big stick to beat them off with before she comes of age. He had been following her around ever since they had been introduced. If Lucas persisted, she would have to ask Drusilla if his attentions were welcome or not.

In a rare quiet moment, Genevieve directed Gideon's attention to the children's table because she had noticed tension between Jayla and Zack's wards.

Gideon sighed. "I'm afraid they didn't hit it off well," he admitted. "Jayla has had such a different upbringing, and there were several incidents—just childish nonsense really, but I'm afraid I don't know much about handling young girls so I expect I wasn't as sympathetic as she thought I should be."

"Well, when we arrive at Glass Castle, I'm sure we can find some young ladies who share more of her interests," she said reassuringly. "In the meantime, perhaps she can accompany Drusilla into city when she is checking on the riverboat loads. Drusilla is older than Jayla, but it might serve."

He smiled at her. "Thank you. I confess I am getting to my wits end in dealing with her."

About an hour after the ceremonies had been concluded and the children sent to their rooms, a soft chime sounded. All the brides rose, each handing their groom a small crystal projecting a map to their quarters.

"Give us about twenty minutes or so to prepare before you gentlemen start for the house," Genevieve told Gideon. "Our efficient Drusilla has seen to it that each crystal will take you to the right room," she added as she followed Katherine and Corrine out of the pavilion.

New Beginnings

AS GENEVIEVE undressed slowly, she could feel the Payome kicking in causing slow warmth to build between her legs and her nipples felt swollen and sensitive. She picked up the negligee laid out on the bed. The gift of the gowns to all the brides had been her idea, but Drusilla had declared that there was nothing suitable in stores so she had designed them. Genevieve had been busy with Parliament, so other than approving the material and expense of sewing, and knowing Drusilla was a skilled designer she had left the creation of the gowns in her baby sister's hands. Now Genevieve picked up hers and her mouth dropped open. Great Goddess! Her sixteen-year-old baby sister had designed *this*?

The material slid sensuously through her hands and along her body as she slipped it on. The loose gown was so thin it felt and looked like a green film and it clung to her skin showing every curve she had. The back started just above her buttocks, the deep vee in front went all the way to her navel and the split on both sides went more than halfway up her thighs. Hastily she picked up the matching robe and donned it. Looking in the mirror, she realized ruefully that the robe's translucent material didn't really make much of an improvement towards modesty.

As the door opened and Gideon entered, she caught a brief glimpse of Vernal passing with his head averted. The door slid closed behind Gideon, but he just stood transfixed, running his eyes over her. She could see him swallow and as his heated gaze rose to meet hers and she could feel herself blushing.

"Drusilla designed the gown and robe. All the brides got one. I'm going to have to ask her where she got the idea for the design—"I'm babbling, she thought. What is wrong with me?

Gideon moved forward slowly, raising a hand to thread his fingers through her unbound hair. "You look beautiful. Your hair is like fire," he said.

"Umm, you like red hair?" she

asked inanely. Her prior experience with a man under the influence of Payome led her to expect their first encounter was going to be fast and a little rough.

Gideon surprised her. "Yes, I like your hair," he said, sliding his hands softly down her arms and bringing her fingers up to his mouth, pressing a kiss on them before laying them on the front of his shirt.

"Why don't you help me undress," he suggested, moving his hands back up to her shoulders and neck so he could cup her face for a kiss. The kiss was gentle and soft, giving her plenty of time to accustom herself to his mouth.

Obediently, Genevieve found herself sliding the buttons open on his shirt and pushing it off his shoulders even as she felt her lips parting for him. As Gideon continued his slow, gentle assault on her senses, she felt a deep, powerful need began to build. Subliminally she knew part of the sexual heat she was feeling was due to the Payome, but it had been years since she had been with a man, and her body was waking up and remembering feelings she thought she had put away forever.

Gideon's skin was slightly rough under her hands, and a light sprinkling of blond hair on his chest made its way down his stomach, disappearing into his trousers. She felt the urge to see and feel more of him, but hesitated to begin to unfasten his pants, so instead she moved closer to him, sliding her arms around his neck and returning his kiss.

As their bodies touched, she could feel the iron control he was exercising to keep from moving too fast for her. When her hips touched his, she felt his arousal and he made a deep guttural sound of pleasure. For just an instant his control slipped, the kiss deepened and his hand tightened on her buttocks, pressing her harder against his swollen shaft.

Not completely in control after all, Genevieve thought naughtily, reaching for the fastening of his trousers.

The climax of their lovemaking was series of fierce and intense waves of pleasure. Afterward, when he collapsed atop her she could still feel faint tremors of pleasure running through her. Absently, she ran her hand through his thick waves blond hair and he turned to look at her anxiously. His expression relaxed when he saw she was smiling faintly at him.

"I think I saw some wine and finger foods on the terrace under a stasis field if you're hungry," Genevieve said.

"Not for food," Gideon said.

"Me neither," Genevieve admitted, reaching for him, wondering if the second time could possibly be as good as the first.

Gorla, her Quirka, woke her just as the sun was rising by bouncing off the balcony rail onto her pillow. Her quills rose as she discovered Gideon sprawled in sleep next to her mistress, but after sniffing his hair, she appeared to accept his presence in Genevieve's bed. The small foxlike pet had disliked Gregor intensely, Genevieve remembered, and the feeling had been mutual.

Carefully so as not to waken her new husband, Genevieve slid out of bed and opened the stasis field long enough to take out a couple of Gorla's favorite finger sandwiches before she made her way to the bathroom. Gorla's fur rippled with pleasure as it changed color to match the food set out.

Putting her hair up to keep it dry, Genevieve eyed her reflection in the mirror. She certainly looked like a woman who had enjoyed her wedding night, she reflected ruefully. Her body was sore in a couple of unaccustomed places too. Strange that Gorla had accepted Gideon so readily, she mused. Comparing the two men was useless because they were so different, Genevieve thought. She was going to have to remember to thank her sister privately for ensuring this relationship was so much better than her last one. Everything about Gideon was different from Gregor not just Gorla's response to him and his to her. Gideon had seemed determined that she should enjoy their sexual encounters as much as he had. Had they really made love four or five times? She couldn't remember Gregor being particularly interested in her reactions to sex at all other than to make sure she was available for it.

Genevieve was so lost in thought she jumped in surprise nearly slipping and falling on the slippery floor when the shower door opened and Gideon stepped in. He caught her against his body, easily keeping her from falling.

"Didn't mean to scare you to death," he said laughing. "I thought we could wash each other's backs."

Genevieve was laughing too. "I'm not used to having company in the shower. I thought you were still asleep and I was trying not to wake you."

"Well, your Quirka wasn't so thoughtful; she wanted more food out of the stasis cube, so she tickled me until I woke up and got it for her. I hope you don't mind. Katherine told us they pretty much eat anything."

"Little glutton; I fed her too," Genevieve said indulgently. She handed him a soapy sponge as he talked, and he began running it over her body.

"Oh, no you don't," Genevieve grabbed a second sponge and began doing the same to him. "You don't get it all your own way this time. I get to play too."

Sailing On The River

ON THE third day after the Handfastings, everyone except for Glass Manor's permanent staff of caretakers, packed up onto five paddlewheel barges and began floating down the river toward Glass Isle. The paddlewheel boats had three decks, two above water and one below to hold cargo. The top deck was the ships control center. On the Second deck were crew and passenger cabins with a long open space in the front. To the front and rear of each boat was a raised platform used as the Dragon Talker station. An outside rail ran the entire length and width of the boat, with a gate opening on the Port side to let down a ramp for loading cargo and passengers. The O'Teague Clan boats were by no means the only traffic in the channel. Small one, two or three man sleds darted about amidst the larger paddlewheel boats. Several independent traders were to be seen sailing both ways, as well as crafts affiliated with various Clans. The Harbor and River Patrols could be seen moving up and down the channel.

The trip to Glass Isle took almost ten days and although each boat was crowded, there a carnival atmosphere among the passengers, with many of the couples taking the opportunity to enjoy the journey as a honeymoon period. Since privacy was at a minimum due to the crowded conditions, there was a lot of talking, laughing and singing. Impromptu games were encouraged. The O'Teague leaders had all elected to travel on the Riverwitch, which was the lead boat. The sisters and aunt took the time to bring each other up to speed on Katherine and Corrine's trip as well as Clan activities. Since there was very little to occupy everyone other than enjoying the scenery, many of the couples took advantage of the enforced idleness to enjoy becoming better acquainted. The Riverwitch only boasted eight passenger cabins besides those occupied by the Captain and her crew and those had been allotted to the O'Teague and her family. The rest of the clan was using pallets on deck at night and occupying foldup chairs during the day. Jayne and the other governesses were kept busy ensuring their charges didn't fall overboard or get in the way of the boat crew as they worked.

As a Dragon Talker, Drusilla was assisting the boat's regular Talker by taking her turn in the front of the boat, ready to ward off any River Nessies who approached too closely. River Nessies lived in large extended family groups with a dominant cow and bull in charge. Unlike the omnivorous Sea Dragons, the herbivorous River Dragons were customarily placid creatures. Although not normally belligerent, their size did make them a hazard to boats plying the channel between islands, and they were nosy creatures, investigating anything new that came their way. The younger bulls could be aggressive in showing off for the females, sometimes causing boats to capsize during their mock battles with each other.

The five ships had just begun the swing around the last two islands in the channel before they began the last leg to Glass Isle. Gideon was standing with Zack and Vernal near the rail. It gave him a good position to watch his new wife as she sat cross-legged on the deck talking to one of Zack's twin boys (he was still having trouble telling them apart). The boy was clutching a basket that Gideon knew held Sooka and Divit,

Katherine and Corrine's Quirkas who were expectant parents.

Zack laughed, giving him a friendly punch on the shoulder. "We can tell where your mind is mate. I bet you he didn't hear a word we just said," he told Vernal.

The older man shook his head mournfully. "No, I'm not giving away my money to you on a sucker's bet like that."

"Hey," Gideon protested. "I was listening." "Right, mate," Zack retorted. "What were we just talking about then?"

Gideon thought fast. "Those," he pointed to the family of Nessies who were swimming slowly across in front of the boat. "We were wondering how long we were going to have to wait on them."

Zack had opened his mouth to reply when the rhythmic sound of the water wheels and the low hum of happy talk was shattered by the scream of several overtaxed engines and the sirens of the River Patrol.

Several watersleds carrying riders and traveling too fast to make the turn raced into the channel and kissed the side of the Riverwitch causing it to rock wildly from side to side. While everyone scrambled not to fall, or for those next to the rail to fall in the water, several more sleds rounded the turn, narrowly missing their careening companions. They were followed by the River Patrol in hot pursuit. The Patrol, being more experienced in traversing the channel at high speed, took the turn fast but in control.

One of the out of control sleds smacked into the rump of a swimming Nessie calf, causing a bellow of pain and fright. Intent on avenging the injury, several infuriated adults turned on the boats. A stream of sticky green goo shot from one Nessie's opened mouth, covering a watersled and its passengers. Screams came from the sled's riders as the acidy goo burned them. A second Nessie sent a large wave of water, swamping not only the sleds, but it caused the Riverwitch to rock wildly back and forth, and the rail to dip dangerously toward the water on both sides. Screams and shouts erupted as people and chairs slid towards the rails and a wave of water soaked everyone on the deck. When the boat righted itself, it tipped dangerously back toward the other side, causing everything to slide in the other direction. Gideon tried to move toward Genevieve and the boy who had been sitting on the deck, but just then, Jayla, arms pinwheeling for balance, crashed into him. Instinctively, he grabbed her with one hand and the rail next to him to keep his balance. He could see that Genevieve was in no danger. She was sitting down with one arm wrapped around the rail stanchion and the other around the boy who was fiercely clutching the basket with the Quirkas. She had caught one of Zack's girls by the back of her shirt with her other hand, keeping the boy and the basket between them.

In the meantime, the Patrol, the fleeing sleds and the Dragons were engaging in a furious three-way battle; the Dragons were bellowing and shooting more goo, the fugitives on the sleds kept firing and dodging in and out wildly and the Patrol was calmly aiming nets at the escaping sleds. Gradually, the fight moved away from the boat, and once the boat ceased rocking so violently Gideon could look for Lucas. He found him at the front of the boat supporting Drusilla as she and the other Talker attempted to calm the Nessies and move them away from the Riverwitch. The Patrol had succeeded in capturing some of the sleds, but a couple had escaped, pursued by some of the Patrol sleds.

The cows had moved the Nessie

calves over to the safety of a small island, and one of them let out a mournful bellow, calling the defenders back to them. Drusilla and Macon, the other Talker, were finally able to *push* hard enough at the two remaining Bull Nessies that they slowly began to shift back toward their herd, still hissing in anger.

Once it was over, Drusilla and the other Talker collapsed, falling ungracefully back on their anchors who sat down hard on the deck to keep either one from hitting her head on the hardwood railing as she went down.

Gideon set Jayla on her feet, and once he ascertained she was unhurt except for being soaked to the knees, he left her and went to check on Genevieve and the two children.

Since they had been sitting on the deck, all three of them were completely soaked with smelly river water. The children seemed to be more worried about the Quirkas whose basket had been drenched than about themselves. Genevieve removed the soaked blankets from the basket and wrung them out, handing them to the boy and telling him to hang them up to dry. She instructed Violet to get some dry ones from Katherine's cabin. "And as soon as you've done that, change into some dry clothes," she called after them as they rushed off with the basket.

Gideon reached down and helped her to her feet. "You could use some dry clothes too," he said.

She pulled her clammy blouse

away from herself and sniffed experimentally. "Ugh. I do stink, don't I?" she said. "I'll change as soon as I can, but I have to make sure no one was hurt before I can worry about how I smell. It's a warm day. A little water won't hurt me. Did you see what happened?"

"Not really, I was too busy fielding Jayla and keeping her and myself from falling overboard. I was worried about you too." He pulled her against him, not caring if she got him wet too.

"Now we're both wet and smelly," Genevieve complained laughing at him.

She stepped back as Katherine, followed by Lucas carrying an unconscious Drusilla headed for the lower wheelhouse.

"What happened?" she asked Corrine, who was following Vernal who was carrying the other Talker.

"I think they just exhausted themselves," Corrine reassured her.

The lower wheelhouse was just a small area with stairs to the upper deck. It had several padded benches and a table for eating. Lucas laid Drusilla down on one and then ordered Riverwitch's captain to bring a glass of water. He knelt beside the bench, rubbing her hands. The captain sent her daughter after two water glasses and then checked on the other Talker who was a crewmember.

"They sure saved our bacon today," she said. She went over to a cabinet and brought out two vials, one of which she handed to Lucas.

"Restorative," she told him. "Give it to her when she comes around."

Katherine inclined her head toward Lucas. "Well," she remarked to Zack, "he's certainly taking charge."

Zack snorted. "Uh-huh. It's wonderful what love will do for a guy."

"What? When? They've known each other less than a week—"

He grinned at her. "Doesn't matter. When it's the right girl, you go down like you were hit by a Robo Tank. I ought to know."

Overhearing, Genevieve protested, "She's only sixteen!"

"So is he," Gideon said mildly. "Maybe we shouldn't let ourselves get all het up over what may prove to be a case of puppy love? She could do a lot worse though."

"It isn't that I don't like him," Genevieve said, "but she's underage—"

Katherine shook her head at her. "Relax Mom," she said, referring to Genevieve having raised Drusilla after their mother passed away. "You weren't much older than she is now when you became Laird. Besides," she added sadly, "a Dragon Talker is never really a child. Before they learn how to shield themselves, a Talker will hear and feel things no child should know about."

At that opportune moment, the Riverwitch Captain reentered with the Patrol Commander who had been chasing the fugitives.

"My Lord, he doesn't recognize

them," she addressed Gideon, "and he would like for you and the others to see if they came to Vensoog on the ship with you."

Security

THEY HAD only been home for a few weeks before it became time for Gideon to attend the quarterly meeting of the Security Council. He reminded Genevieve she had agreed to make the trip with him so they would have more time together without, as he put it, 'feeling like bugs under a microscope'.

"I'm sorry," she said, "Being the center of attention can be a little overwhelming if you aren't used to it. I suppose everyone is using us as a marker to see how well the program Katherine designed is working."

"Well, it's not that I haven't been

in the position of having everyone's eyes on me before, but it wasn't about personal things," he admitted. "I suppose I'll get used to it and I'm sure everyone will find something else to talk about sooner or later. Even without all that, I'd appreciate your input on planetary politics, so I don't accidentally put my foot in things during the meeting," he said.

The first Security Council meeting took place in the afternoon, so while he was tied up meeting all his opposite numbers, Genevieve occupied herself in the archives, entering data concerning the positions the new clan members had taken up.

After Gideon and Genevieve left the Parliamentary Council building, they got into the rear seat of a handy air sled taxi and gave their destination as the O'Teague Manor. Gideon put an arm around her and leaned in as if he was about to kiss her. Instead, he whispered in her ear, "Does this thing have a privacy screen?"

As she reached for it, he instructed, "Giggle like I just said something funny. We want the driver to think we're going to play a little slap and tickle."

Obediently, Genevieve did as he asked. As soon at the privacy screens engaged, Gideon said, "We're not the only Clan that's been having trouble with raiders armed with high tech weapons and who disappear afterwards. Despite some resistance from Ivanov's Grand Duke Gregor the council concluded we have a crew on a Jack ship in orbit doing the raiding."

"Was Lewiston serving as Security for DeMedici?" Genevieve asked.

"Oh, yes. He tried awfully hard to persuade the others we need to consolidate our forces and name a central commander."

"Himself, I assume?"

"Well, he did offer, but when I nominated, Shīfu Mullins from Yang, as coordinator, it went through. Mostly, I think because Ivanov didn't want to establish that much power in Lewiston's hands. I don't see how Lewiston and Ivanov could have gotten acquainted with each other, but I could swear they knew each other before this. Ivanov also poo-pooed the idea that the raids are being coordinated."

"Did you say Gregor Ivanov?"

"Yes, I think that was his first name," he answered.

Genevieve frowned. "I thought the Tsarina booted him out ten years ago after we complained about him leading off planet raiders onto our lands. I suppose after the bio attack the Tsarina welcomed back any of the male bloodline who hadn't been on planet during the outbreak." She looked over at Gideon. "Do you remember me telling you about the guy on my Match List who turned out to be connected to the raiders?"

"That was Ivanov?" he asked.

When she nodded, he looked thoughtful, "Ivanov did everything he could to discourage the idea of the raider's attacks being coordinated. He seemed pretty anxious for the rest of us to think these were just isolated raids. That makes me wonder if he still has ties to them. We knew Lewiston had some unsavory connections; he was suspected of selling military weapons to Space Jacks. If Ivanov used to be with the Jacks, maybe that's where he and Lewiston met."

"You think the two of them are working together?"

Gideon tapped his chin with a finger. "It fits. It fits even better if Ivanov knows about Lewiston's takeover plot but has a different end than Lewiston does. It would explain why he doesn't want Lewiston to be in charge of planetary defense. Okay, I think tomorrow I need to get back to the City and send a message to an old buddy of mine who joined the Patrol after he mustered out. The patrol needs to know there may be a Jack Ship operating in this area of space anyway—"

There was a flash of light and a loud *Whump!* and the front of the taxi exploded. The craft spun end over end and emergency foam erupted into the passenger area. When the sled landed, it skidded over onto one side and slid before smacking into the side of a closed shop. During the crash, although Gideon and Genevieve were somewhat protected by the foam, they still ended up in a heap on the bottom passenger door.

"Genevieve? are you hurt?"

Gideon demanded.

She spat foam out of her mouth, and wiped her eyes. Gorla had managed to avoid being squished by hanging onto the car's Security straps. Genevieve caught her as she jumped down and then wiped her eyes and nose as well. "I'm okay. You?"

"Yeah. We need to get out of here. That was no accident." He levered himself out from under her and stood up on the door. He was too tall to stand upright but he managed to get the other passenger door to open. He boosted himself up onto the side of the cab, and reached down to help the shorter Genevieve climb out.

Although close to the docks, the area consisted of small shops and some warehouses. Surprisingly, the noise of the crash had not drawn a crowd. There was no one around and all the shops had closed for the day. Probably the owners lived above them, but if so, they weren't coming out to help.

Glancing around for where the shot might have come from, Gideon could see several possibilities. He grabbed Genevieve's hand and pulled her into the closest alley.

When she protested at leaving the driver, he said, "She's gone. We need to get away from here. Now."

"The Patrol—" Genevieve began.

"Aren't here," Gideon finished. "But whoever shot at us may be here waiting to check for survivors. Move, woman."

Sure enough, as they ran down

the alley, they heard voices coming from the street. Gideon hastily shoved Genevieve behind him into an overhanging doorway. The door didn't give when he tested it, but he hoped the darkened entranceway would prevent their attackers from seeing them. He drew the sidearm he wore like a second skin and waited. Behind him, he could feel Genevieve wiggling to the side in attempt to give him more room to hide.

He thrust and arm across her waist, and muttered, "Stop moving! Movement draws attention."

Obediently, she stilled.

One of the men came down the alleyway, gun drawn.

"See anything?" one of the other two at the mouth of alley called.

"No, I don't think they came this way."

"Come on back then. The door was open so we know they got out. They have to be around here somewhere."

As the third man passed them going back to the street, the door behind Gideon and Genevieve was shoved open, spilling them out into the alley. "Hey!" the shop owner yelled, "Who's out there?"

"There they are!" yelled one of the men at the front of the alley. The light from the open door clearly revealed Gideon and Genevieve. The men raised weapons and began firing.

"Genevieve run! I'll follow you," Gideon ordered. He was annoyed when she ignored his command, pulling her Force Wand as she stepped up beside him. Roughly, he shoved her back behind him with his left hand as he fired with his right. Genevieve made a small 'ooof!' sound as she hit the ground, but he couldn't spare the time to check on her. He tucked and rolled, firing again as he did. He felt the heat of the three men's pulsars as plasma bolts shot through where he had just been standing. One of the attackers was down not moving, and a second was moaning in pain as he clutched his leg where Gideon's bolt had hit him. The third man ignored Gideon and aimed behind him in the direction Genevieve had fallen. Gideon's next shot took off the top of his head, but he heard the man's plasma bolt sizzle at it hit the wall.

The dark alley made it impossible to know if Genevieve had been hit. Stern discipline, born of surviving countless battles, made Gideon pause to check and see if any of the men were still a threat before he turned to check on Genevieve. The shop owner had wisely ducked back inside his dwelling and Genevieve was staggering to her feet. Gideon gripped her arm and yanked her the rest of the way upright, causing Gorla, who was still clinging to her shoulder, to squeak indignantly. "Didn't I tell you to run?" he demanded furiously. "Woman, when we're in a fight like this I expect my orders to be obeyed!"

Genevieve glared right back at him. "I'm not one of your soldiers! I don't take orders from you!"

He gave her a slight shake. "When it comes to your personal safety, you damn will obey my orders or I'll turn you over my knee, understand?"

She opened her mouth to shout back at him and he could see an aureole of blue sparks beginning to build around her head. Gorla chirped at her and tugged on her hair. She blew out a long breath, and he could practically see her reining in her temper.

"I realize, Lord Gideon," she said with icy quiet, "that your intemperate tone is due to concern for my safety, but you need to learn that the O'Teague doesn't run away leaving others to fight my battles."

"And you need to learn, that in the heat of battle, I may not have time to explain why I give an order, so I repeat, I expect to be obeyed when I give one," his voice was equally cold and formal.

As furious Gideon was with her, he found himself distracted by the blue sparks floating around her hair. Gingerly, he reached out to touch them, got zapped with a small electric shock and jerked back. Holstering his gun, he took her hand and led her toward the mouth of the alley. "C'mon, we need to get out of here and back to Glass Manor. We can finish this discussion later."

Genevieve followed him in silence. Finally, she let out a small huff of breath. "I really hate it when I'm wrong. I would have gotten in your way, wouldn't I?"

"Yep. You aren't carrying a gun

and however lethal that wand is in close combat, it's no good as a distance weapon," he said flatly.

"I'm sorry I didn't consider that. I tend to react badly when I'm yelled at," she added.

His curiosity got the better of his temper. "How did you do that thing with the sparks? Do you know it bit me like free electricity when I touched it?"

"You could see it?" she asked. "Most off-worlders don't have enough Psy to do so. I'm not sure exactly what causes it. It just always shows up when I get really angry."

Gideon said nothing because his own body's intemperate reaction to the adrenaline surge from the fight was making it difficult to focus on the situation at hand. He knew they still might be in danger from whoever had sent their attackers. He didn't need to glance down to be aware of his fierce arousal. His trained fighter's reflexes and discipline prevented him from reacting to his body's urgent demands.

He had again been caught by surprise by Genevieve. Accustomed as he was to spoiled beauties like his deceased sister-in-law, the ladies of Vensoog continually responded to situations differently than his expectations. Katherine, he remembered, had not only jumped into a deadly encounter with a group of hardened thugs to protect a pack of children she was barely acquainted with, but she had taken out two of them to his and Zack's one each.

In the two months since the Handfasting, he had found himself continually blindsided by Genevieve's behavior and his own response to it. Gideon's primary experience with non-military women had been his lovely, spoiled and selfish sister-in-law and her friends who wouldn't have taken a step out of their way unless it benefited them on a personal basis. He had enjoyed their company but he had never experienced anything more than a mild pleasure in it. Unconsciously, he had expected the same feelings from his new marriage. In Genevieve's place, his dead sister-in-law or one of her friends would have been complaining and blaming him for her discomfort. The idea that Celia could have reined in her temper the way Genevieve had was absurd. He certainly couldn't imagine any of the women he had known being soaked with smelly river water or doused with emergency foam without raising a major fuss. Yet Genevieve had endured both these things not only without complaint, but she had put the discomfort aside in favor of more urgent matters.

Even though Gideon had been given an image of Genevieve when Katherine announced the matches back on Fenris and he had been prepared for her looks, he hadn't been ready for the shock of desire that hit him when he encountered the warmth of her smile and seen the kindness with which she had greeted Lucas and Jayla. She had explained away Jayla's poor behavior with empathy and certainly made it seem less like that of a spoiled brat and more like that of a child in pain needing comfort and reassurance. Longer acquaintance had proved her both smart and kind, with a quirky sense of humor and a sunny disposition.

On their wedding night, Gideon had intended to offer to wait to consummate the marriage until they had a chance to get to know each other better. The sight of Genevieve waiting for him had aroused such a flood of desire that it had driven everything but the fact that she was his and she was willing out of his head.

"I think the Patrol finally got here," Genevieve remarked into the silence when they arrived back at the scene of the accident. A single rider airsled and a larger sled for transport marked with the Security Council Patrol insignia were parked next to the destroyed taxi and three officers were examining the wreck.

Seeing them covered in emergency foam, the officer in charge immediately identified them as having been in the sled when it crashed.

"Who are you and what happened here?" she asked.

After identifying themselves, Gideon explained that they had been attacked. He indicated that two of the attackers were dead in the alley behind them and that one of them might still be alive.

Vensoog's system of rotating the responsibility for Port Recovery's government between the clans did have its advantages, Gideon mused, remembering a similar incident on Fenris when Katherine had been attacked by thugs from the Thieves Guild. That time they had spent the rest of the night in a police station answering questions. Although plainly unhappy with the situation, the Vensoog officer agreed to provide them with a ride to Glass Manor and to let them put off making a statement until the next day. Gideon supposed that since control of the City Patrol rotated between clans on a yearly basis, line officers might be wary of annoying Genevieve unnecessarily. Clan

O'Teague held the Security chair this year, which made Gideon their de facto boss. Even though he would not have interfered with how the Patrol functioned, they didn't know that. The men who killed the taxi driver were either dead or wounded and headed for the Patrol infirmary so there was no real urgency to keep Genevieve and Gideon tied up all night giving statements.

The next morning Genevieve's com chimed as they were leaving to make their statements at the Patrol station, "You go ahead," she told Gideon. "It's Drusilla. I suppose she has a question about something to do with the storm preparations. I want to stop at the armory and pick up a gun anyway."

"I'll meet you at the boat dock,"

he said as he left.

"Are you alone?" Drusilla asked as her image popped up.

"Yes. Gideon just left. Why?" Genevieve said.

"It's about Jayla and I wanted to talk to you and let you decide how much to tell Gideon."

Genevieve's eyebrows rose. "What's the matter?"

"Well, she's—she's acting funny. If I thought she could have met anyone this soon, I would swear she's sneaking out to meet someone we wouldn't approve of."

"Sneaking out? Don't you think that's a little over the top?"

"Well, that's just it. Yesterday she was supposed to be at her self-defense lesson and she told the instructor she had a headache and was going to lie down. When I went by her room to check on her, she was gone. I happened to glance out the window and I saw her riding away."

"I see," Genevieve said thoughtfully. "Well, I don't think we need to panic yet, but do keep an eye on her. You might ask if there are any strangers hanging around the castle. We had an incident last night, and Gideon has put some new security procedures in place. Please pass along the warning to all the outlying farms and Islands."

"Okay, I can do that. I just wanted you to know about Jayla," Drusilla said, signing off.

On the way to the armory, Genevieve found herself wondering, as Drusilla had, what the child could be up to. As far as she could tell, Jayla hadn't made any new friends among the castle or town folk. If she was sneaking out to meet someone, it had to be someone she had met here in town.

When she entered the armory, she found Marjorie, the weapons clerk, engaged in a snarky argument concerning the new weapons and sleds Gideon had ordered that morning.

"Lord Gideon ordered them and he wants them soonest!" Marjorie told the woman on the other end of the vid screen.

Listening quietly, Genevieve picked up a light shoulder harness and plasma gun and strapped them on. She also selected a small boot knife and sheath.

"And I'm telling you," the accountant retorted snippily, "that the O'Teague hasn't okayed these orders. I can't put them through until she does."

"But he's Warlord!" Marjorie protested. "This is what he's supposed to do."

"I don't care what he's supposed to do! What do we know about these men anyway? They can't just come in and take over. Nobody's even trying to find a cure anymore!" Abruptly, she shut off the screen.

Marjorie looked over at Genevieve. "Sorry about that Milady. Let me sign those out to you."

A tall, light haired man Genevieve recognized as one of Gideon's unit looked up from a plastia sheet he had been studying. He was Marjorie's new husband and he was just coming off his shift. "Was that Grace in procurement? She's been giving Bobbie down in sled maintenance grief about the same thing," he offered.

Marjorie warily eyed the blue sparks that had begun to appear around Genevieve's hair.

"Umn, that's Grace down in purchasing," she called as Genevieve turned and stalked out the door.

"I wish I was a bug on the wall down there," she remarked to her new husband.

"Why?" he asked.

"Did you see those blue sparks the O'Teague was giving off? Anytime they appear, it's time to duck and cover."

"Well, I did see some kind of halo or something around her as she left. What are they?"

Marjorie grinned at him. "It's a kind of aura that shows up under strong emotions. Most off-worlders don't have enough Psy to see them. I'm glad you do. When the O'Teague sparks blue, it means she's getting ready to blow. I bet we have some of this stuff by this afternoon."

Genevieve slapped open the door where the Manor's offices were kept and stood there with her fists on her hips. "I'm looking for Grace," she announced.

"Can I help you, M'Lady?" asked an older woman coming hastily forward.

"Dora, you aren't Grace,"

Genevieve replied.

The woman eyed the sparks, which had intensified around Genevieve's head warily. "No, but I'm in charge here."

Genevieve looked at her. "Dora," she said pleasantly, "Please assemble your staff for a brief meeting immediately and make sure this Grace attends."

"Okay, everyone, please come to the front of the room for a brief meeting with the O'Teague," Dora called.

Genevieve waited, tapping her foot impatiently. "Dora, you seem to have some new staff since the last time I was in here. Please introduce them to me."

Once introductions were made, Genevieve nodded pleasantly to the gathered workers. "You may or may not be aware," she remarked, "that last night on the way home from the Security Council meeting, an attempt was made to kill the Warlord and myself."

She waited while the buzz of exclamations died down. "Since we don't know at this point if the attack was aimed directly at us or at the clan in general, Lord Gideon has implemented some new procedures for our safety. I know you will all cooperate in these new measures. Thank you."

As the crowd started to move away, Genevieve said, "Just a minute Grace. I understand there seems to be some problem with Lord Gideon's signature. I was under the impression we had taken care of that the day he arrived."

"No, we have a copy on file," Grace said sulkily.

"Really," Genevieve purred, moving into Grace's personal space and staring her down, "then perhaps you can tell me why you're requiring me to sign off on his orders?"

"It was a misunderstanding," Grace muttered, backing away.

"I certainly hope so," Genevieve stated. "Lord Gideon is an experienced battle leader. Following his orders will keep us all safer. I hope I don't find it necessary to revisit this matter, Grace. Are we clear on that?"

"Yes, Milady," Grace's voice was submissive, but her eyes glared defiance before she turned away.

Genevieve looked after her a

moment longer before she turned to Dora. "I'm reading more than officiousness here. What is her problem?"

"I'm sorry, Milady. Her little brother was one of those affected by the weapon. He lived, but she can't accept that we can't cure him and she is very bitter about it."

"I see," Genevieve said. "Well, I'm sorry her brother was hurt, but everything we could do has been done. In the meantime, I recommend you move her into a job that won't bring her into conflict with the new clan members. I also suggest she needs to see a counselor. If there is an issue about payment, let her know the clan will pay for it."

Dora nodded. "As you will

Milady."

Genevieve acknowledge the nod and left. She was very thoughtful as she walked down to the boat dock to meet Gideon. Here she found another controversy brewing. The large water sled was docked and several clan members were waiting to board. Leanne, one of the botanists in charge of the Manors gardens was confronting Gideon.

"I don't like guns," she protested, "so I don't carry one. I don't see as it's necessary to go armed to shop for vegetable seeds."

"Until we know if the attack last night was specific to Genevieve and myself or aimed generally at the clan," Gideon said patiently, "no one is to leave the safety of the grounds without carrying a gun. And we need to travel in mixed pairs or threesomes."

"And if I refuse to carry one?" Leanne challenged.

"Then you won't leave the Manor," Gideon replied simply.

Leanne glared at him. She spotted Genevieve watching the encounter and asked angrily, "Do I have to do this?"

Genevieve pinched her nose between her fingers and sighed. "Lord Gideon knows very much more about how to keep us all out of danger than we do," she reminded everyone listening. "The Clan will all be much safer if we listen to him and cooperate with these new safety precautions. Leanne," she said reasonably, "think how you will feel if a clan member or an innocent bystander is hurt because you disobeyed orders. Now Marjorie has a few of these light weight plasma guns like what I'm wearing left in the armory and expects more to come in this afternoon."

"Stop being such an ass, Leanne," one of the men said. "Let's go get your gun. I promise it won't poison you."

"Thank you," Gideon said softly when Genevieve went over to him and leaned her head against his shoulder.

"Why is none of this ever easy?" she wondered, "I warned Drusilla to increase security precautions and she is going to pass it along to the outposts as well. I just wish we knew what to look out for."

"Me too," he responded.

Clan Honor

THE INTERVIEW at the City Patrol station took most of the morning. When asked if they knew who had attacked them, Gideon and Genevieve looked at each other. "Let's just say that we have our suspicions," Gideon said carefully. "However, since all we have is suspicion we don't intend to make an accusation at this time."

The investigative officer, Detective Ramirez, scowled at them. "My Lord, may I remind you that the Council employs us to investigate these matters? It would be much better if you would allow us to do our jobs."

"Without proof," Genevieve put in gently, "all an accusation now would do is spark anger between the Clans. I'm sure that none of us wants to arouse another Clan Feud. Once we have proof, I promise you we will come to you, won't we, Milord."

"Sure," Gideon agreed. "We'll keep you in the loop."

Ramirez eyed Gideon skeptically, aware that he had not agreed they would come to her to make an arrest, only that they would keep her informed.

"Do you have an address for our slain driver?" Genevieve asked as she rose. "I would like to pay a condolence call on the family."

"I'm sure they can give you that out front," Ramirez said. "If you will stay a moment Lord Gideon, I will give you my contact information."

Gideon had given instructions that the large air shuttle used to transport clan members to the City landing docks remain in the city with them. As he had pointed out to Genevieve, it was large enough to accommodate most of the people wanting to go into the city and it had the virtue of being equipped with a force field in case they were attacked. The driver and one additional security person were to remain with it at all times. Everyone who had used it for transport was told to return to the city passenger wharf before dusk that evening. There had been some grumbles but seeing he had Genevieve's backing, the Clan didn't fight him.

When they came out of the City Patrol station, he directed the shuttle to the local Space Patrol office so he could send off his message concerning the rogue ship and crew. By the time the message had been sent off, it was almost noon.

"What part of the city are you going to?" asked Gideon, referring to Genevieve's plan to offer condolences to the late taxi driver's family.

"I will be going to the City Child Care office," she replied. "It seems our taxi drivers only relatives were two small girls without a clan attachment. The case worker Toni Lewellyn tells me that the mother arrived with a baby and a toddler less than a year before the war ended."

"You are planning on bringing them home with us aren't you," he asked perceptively.

"Without a Clan to take them in, they will be at the mercy of whomever the City chooses to raise them. Their mother was in our service when she was killed, Gideon."

She discovered her husband was studying her with a peculiar look on his face. "What?" she asked. "Why are you looking at me like that? Do I have a smut on my face or something?"

"No," he said smiling. "There is not a thing wrong with you."

He pretended to turn a deaf ear when he heard one of his men mutter to the other, "Boss is going down for the third time, isn't he?"

"What do you mean going?" the other one snorted. "I'd say he's gone."

When he attempted to leave all the security guards they had brought with them with Genevieve, she objected.

"I seem to recall someone insisting that all of us travel with at least one companion," Genevieve reminded him. "You can't expect the clan to obey you if you don't follow your own orders, you know."

"I won't need security," he told her. "I am going to be inside the Council Chambers. You are the one who will be out and around town."

"All the same, I will feel much better if you take someone to watch your back," she said. "Besides, I don't trust Lewiston. He knows you are the greatest threat to his plans, not me. If he starts a fight inside the chamber, he could take the opportunity to make sure you didn't make it out of there. It wouldn't be the first time someone was assassinated during a Security Council meeting. If you have someone with you, I won't worry so much. Please?"

He looked at her in exasperation. By putting it on a personal basis, she had cut his argument off at the knees. Still, he tried again, "Genevieve that's flattering, but I'm not the only experienced soldier O'Teague has. Lewiston has no more reason to be afraid of me than he has Zack or Vernal, or any number of trained leaders."

"Yes he does," she insisted, "you're better than he is and he knows it and he's afraid of you. I saw the way he watched you when got off the shuttle that first day. Please?"

"Alright," he sighed. "Jorgensen, you're with me. The meeting should be over by four thirty. You can return and pick me up then," he told the shuttle driver. He brushed a light kiss on Genevieve's cheek and the two men got out of the shuttle and went up the steps to the Security Council headquarters, a double-stack dome that had been one of the first buildings put up by the settlers. Ornate carvings of each clan's symbol were cut into the double entry doors.

As the shuttle door closed, Mira,

one of the remaining Security personnel, looked over at her Laird and said dryly, "Laid it on a little thick there, didn't you ma'am?"

Genevieve banged the back of her head on her headrest. "Oh, Goddess," she moaned. "I've turned into my mother! I can't believe I did that."

Mira started laughing. "Well," she choked out, "sweet reason does get you what you want more than shouting and stamping—"

"Oh, shut up," the O'Teague said. "You wait, you'll come to it too and when you do, I'm going to be the one laughing."

Rick, the other security guard, being male, didn't get the joke. "Somebody want to fill me in here?" he asked.

This set off a fresh spasm of wails from both women.

It was a good thing this trip had started out with laughter, Genevieve thought, because Marylou Heron, the slain taxi driver had no family other than the two little girls who were currently in the custody of the City Child Care office.

"Heron apparently didn't have any clan affiliations," Toni Lewellyn, the Case Worker informed Genevieve. "She arrived on Vensoog about three years ago just before that damn bio-virus went off. We think she was a refugee in transit, but we don't know from what planet. Her passport just says, 'in transit'. We found the children's birth records in her papers, but she listed the father as deceased."

"You did run their DNA though the clan database? Even if was a generation or so back—"

Lewellyn shook her head slowly in negation. "No, whoever he was the father didn't have Vensoog ties either. There's something else too. The girl's DNA is—odd."

"Odd?" Genevieve questioned. "Odd as in not quite human?"

"No, they're human alright, but the DNA code was perfect. No anomalies at all."

"So, they're healthy. Why is that a problem? Oh, you think their DNA was tampered with?"

"Well, if it was tampered with, it was several generations back. The mothers was the same."

Genevieve looked over at the little girls who were occupied playing with some toys the Center furnished, and paying no attention to the adults who were deciding their fate.

"It doesn't matter. Their mother was in our service when she was killed," Genevieve said. "They have family now. Will it be possible to take them with us this afternoon?"

Lewellyn, smiled at her, holding out a crystal. "I was hoping you would say that. I have the paperwork with me now. Clan O'Teague has the reputation of taking care of its own so I took the liberty of preparing it."

Genevieve touched the crystal, adding her DNA signature to the encoded document.

Rick looked over at Mira. "Just like that, she takes them in because they have no one else? The woman only drove a cab for her once."

"Heron was in service with us at the time she was killed," Genevieve told him kindly. "Even if I was willing to turn my back on two helpless babies, Clan honor would require me to take them in. You'll learn our ways soon enough."

"Not all the Clans are so scrupulous," Lewellyn remarked.

Genevieve ignored her, walked over to the girls, and sat down on the floor with them. "Hello," she said. "My name is Genevieve. What's yours?"

The elder of the two dark-haired moppets answered her. "My name is Ceridwen and this is my sister Bronwen."

"Those are lovely names. I'm so

sorry about your mother, Ceridwen. My husband and I were riding in her taxi when she died. She was a brave woman. You can be very proud of her."

"Thank you," Ceridwen replied gravely. "We are."

"Do you remember your mother telling you about your family, aunts or uncles maybe?"

"She said there was just us," Ceridwen replied.

"We had Oona," Bronwen spoke for the first time.

"Who is Oona?" Genevieve asked.

"Our Quirka, like her," said Ceridwen, pointing to Gorla who held her usual perch on Genevieve shoulder. "She ran away when she came for us."

"She wouldn't let us look for her,"

said Bronwen, pointing her chin at Lewellyn.

"Was that at your home?" Genevieve asked.

"Yes," Lewellyn answered. "They had quite a fit when the little critter ran off, but it was the middle of the night and it was dark. The old woman who was watching them said she would keep an eye out for her."

"We will go back to your home and look for her," Genevieve promised. "Your Quirka is a part of your family and it is very important that family members stick together. Your mother was in my service when she died. That means you are now part of my family and it is now my job to look after you. When we leave here, we'll go back to where you were living and collect Oona and anything else you want to take with you. You are going to be living with me now and become a part of Clan O'Teague."

"Do you hit?" asked Bronwen.

Genevieve smiled. "I don't hit little girls even when they misbehave. That doesn't mean there won't be rules you will be expected to obey, but I will always explain them to you before I ask you to obey them."

She stood up and held out her hands to the girls. "Are you ready to come with me?"

After a brief hesitation, the girls took her hands. "I'm hungry," announced Bronwen.

"Well, then let's go and eat some lunch before we go and find Oona."

When they picked up Gideon and

his companion in front of the City offices, he was not surprised to discover that his immediate family had been increased by two small girls and another Quirka.

Jorgensen had been right, earlier, he reflected. As far as his feelings for Genevieve went, he had gone down for the last time. The two little girls sitting shyly in the seats beside Genevieve had been the final blow to resisting his love for her. He just needed to convince her to make their bond permanent. There was no rush, he assured himself. He had a whole year to convince her to stay married to him.

Genevieve would have preferred to stay home with the girls on their first evening, but the heads of Clan O'Teague were expected at a soiree given by Clan Yang at their city headquarters that evening. Genevieve arranged for Mira to stay with the girls until she and Gideon returned.

Like Glass Manor, Yang Palace had been built right after the founders landed, and like Glass Manor, it had been considerably renovated by the Clan over the past two hundred years. Although Clan Yang had kept the domed façade on the outside, inside the structure had been remodeled to resemble the Chinese Emperor's palace on Old Earth. What had been the common room now sported dozens of statues of Chinese dragons and ancient warriors along the walls, and the floor itself had been retiled with granite resembling marble.

Genevieve and Gideon paused in the doorway to greet their hosts Nü-Huang Toshi Ishamara and her consort Shīfu Mike Mullins. Nü-Huang Toshi was a tiny woman with almost blue-black hair just now swept up into an elaborate hairstyle and wearing traditional Chinese Robes. Her Shīfu, Mike Mullins, was dressed in the traditional outfit of an eighteenth-century warlord, and despite the incongruence of his name, he looked the part.

"I'm in awe at how beautiful this is every time I come here," Genevieve told Toshi.

"Well, it does help to remind the Clan of our origins," Toshi remarked. She smiled at Gideon, "Mike still isn't sure whether to thank you for nominating him to oversee any planetary military defense we might need, Lord Gideon."

"On the contrary," the Shīfu remarked, "I'm pretty sure he handed me a hot potato."

Gideon laughed. "Nonsense, I'm sure you will handle the job with your usual finesse. Besides, there for a minute it looked as if Lewiston might manage to get himself elected and I know you didn't want that any more than I did."

"Well, we appreciated the information you passed on to us aboard ship about the weapons drop," Mullins said. "I did manage to verify that a cargo drop was made to an island between DeMedici and O'Teague just after we arrived. Have you learned anything more?"

Toshi sighed. "That seems to be

all our men want to talk about tonight. Genevieve, the buffet is excellent. Tonight, we're serving some traditional delicacies brought in by the Dancing Gryphon. Let us go and indulge while they gossip about past deeds."

"The buffet table looks wonderful," Genevieve said, as they moved away. "Your people have done a great job."

Toshi had the right idea, Genevieve thought. A social event such as this had enabled her to meet with the other clan leaders and discuss ideas for countering the raiders and setting up a communications system to enable each clan leader to know which area had been raided last which would help establish if a pattern of the raids could be seen.

She was coming back from the lady's room with her mind on these things when a tall, well-built, dark haired man stepped into her path. His too handsome face was a little marred by a scar near his eyebrow. Otherwise, he hadn't changed much. "Hello Love, did you miss me?" Gregor Ivanov asked.

Startled, Genevieve took an involuntary step backward but her voice was cool. "Hello Gregor. I see you managed to get your sister to forgive you. Does she know about your ties to the raiders?"

He laughed, moving in closer. She didn't like it but she felt another retreat would be a sign of weakness.

"I'm a reformed man, didn't you hear?"

Genevieve looked him up and down. "I could say I have waterfront property on Sahara to sell too, but that wouldn't make it the truth."

She started to move past him and he caught her arm. "Oh love, now don't be that way. It could still be good between us. Don't you remember how good it was?"

"No, I don't," Genevieve retorted. "Let go, Gregor". She tried to pull her arm free and his fingers tightened painfully. She was going to have bruises tomorrow, she knew.

"Maybe you need reminding," he began, attempting to draw her back to him.

"And maybe she doesn't," Gideon said pleasantly. His hand clamped down on Gregor's wrist, and Gregor gave a gasp of pain and released Genevieve who immediately moved to Gideon's side.

An ugly look came into Gregor's eyes. "I hear you're some hotshot strategist, Michaels. Smart enough to get picked as a husband to one of the Clan leaders anyway."

"I was very lucky Katherine's program picked such a wonderful woman for my wife," Gideon agreed, his voice still pleasant. He put an arm possessively around Genevieve who snuggled up against him. To annoy Gregor, she cast an adoring look up at Gideon, who didn't notice because he was too busy watching Gregor the way a Quirka watched for house vermin to come out of hiding.

"Genevieve I'm surprised. Who

would have thought a little rebel like you would be impressed by a big war hero," Gregor sneered.

"Your sister has given you a second chance, Gregor," Genevieve said, ignoring the insult. "I suggest you make the most of it and forget the past. I have." She looked up at Gideon again. "I don't want to leave the girls alone too long on their first night with us. Are you ready?"

"Yes. I thought you might be willing to leave by now so I looked for you," he said, not taking his eyes off Gregor.

"Yes," she agreed. "Let's say goodnight to our hosts and leave, shall we?"

"Anytime, Darling," Gideon said, still watching Gregor, who glared back at him.

"We'll finish our conversation some other time love," he said to Genevieve over his shoulder as he left.

"No thank you," she snapped, finally losing her temper. "Go back and play in your sandbox, Gregor. I may not have been able to tell the difference between spoiled boys and real men ten years ago, but I can assure you, the difference is obvious now."

Gideon looked at the sparkling blue halo surrounding her hair and laughed.

"I'm afraid I've made you an enemy," she said to Gideon as they watched Gregor retreating.

"I've had enemies before. He doesn't worry me," he said.

Despite his mild words, Gideon made love to her fiercely that night, almost as if he was trying to imprint himself on her. Afterward, pleasantly tired, she laid her head on his shoulder, drifting towards sleep. He touched the finger shaped bruises forming on her arm with a gentle finger.

"Ivanov do that?" he asked frowning.

She smiled a little. "I'll heal. You probably did worse to him when you grabbed his wrist to make him let go."

"He was acting a little like a jealous ex-lover," he said. "Is he likely to make more trouble?"

She sat up to pull her nightgown back on." What do you mean?"

Gideon shifted so he was propped

up on the headboard. "You said you were the one who ended the relationship. Jealousy can make a man do stupid things, like come after you to hurt you," he said mildly.

Genevieve cast him a suspicious look from under her lashes, wondering if he was as calm as he sounded. She was learning that with Gideon a mild voice might not reflect his true feelings.

She shook her head. "Well, he was pretty angry at me for ruining his plans, but I don't fool myself there was anything personal about it. I was a means to an end. He's not like you—people are tools to him."

She moved so they were again lying against each other, running her hand down the hard muscles in his chest. "If you're having trouble falling asleep, we could do something else," she suggested.

He caught her hand before it could go lower and brought it up to his mouth. "You shouldn't have gotten dressed again."

At breakfast the next day, she informed Gideon that she needed to take the children shopping for some new clothes before they returned home.

He frowned at her. "What's wrong with what they are wearing now?"

"Gideon," she said patiently, "it's practically all they have. What other clothes they own is either worn-out or too small. While I'm sure that we have clothing to fit them back at Glass Castle, it isn't new. I think they need just a few new things so they don't feel like a charity case."

"Take at least two security personnel with you," he reminded her.

"In that case, may I have Mira and Marjorie?"

"Why them in particular?" he asked.

Genevieve smiled at him. "Because my dear, they're women; I've yet to meet a man who enjoys clothes shopping. Your male security officers won't appreciate me inflicting a shopping trip on any them. Unless of course you would like to go with us?"

"No that's fine," he said hastily. "I'll make sure the day supervisor knows to assign them to you."

Both security women laughed

heartily when she described the story to them. It had been some time since Genevieve had indulged herself in a girl's day out and Mira and Marjorie were good companions. As they came out of the fourth store however, she noticed that both women were carefully scrutinizing everyone on the walkway.

"What is it?" she asked, drawing the girls closer.

"Not sure," Mira said softly, "but we think we're being followed."

"Let's take a break at that Cafka shop over there and watch the crowd for a little while. Maybe the girls are ready for some ices?" Marjorie suggested.

They seated Genevieve and the girls between them at a table next to the wall. A young pleasant faced girl came to take their order. The café was one of the few who still used a live server instead of an autobot that looked human. While Genevieve ordered, Mira directed Marjorie's attention to the tall dark man standing across the street.

"Is that who you saw earlier?" she asked.

"Yes. He looks familiar. I wonder where I've seen him. Maybe one of us should go and ask him why he's been following us around."

"I don't think we'll have to," Mira said. "He's coming inside."

Genevieve looked up from fastening a bib on Bronwen to keep her from dripping ice cream on her shirt.

"Well, Dragon Crap," she said.

"Do you recognize him Milady?"

Mira asked.

Genevieve was annoyed. "Unfortunately, I do. His name is Gregor Ivanov. He's Grand Duke for Ivanov Clan. Lord Gideon and I had a small skirmish with him at last night's party."

Gregor smiled winningly at the three women as he came up to the table.

"Do you mind if I join you, Ladies?"

Both Marjorie and Mira stood up, hands going to their sidearms.

"Yes, actually, we do," Genevieve said. "Go away, Gregor."

"Oh, come now love," he said, sitting down anyway. "Surely such old friends as we are can forgive a few harsh words. Besides, you don't want to make a scene in front of these nice little girls, do you?"

Genevieve gave him a nasty smile. "Strangely enough, Gregor, I don't mind my new daughters seeing a brawl nearly as much you seem to think I would. We had more than harsh words and I have nothing to say to you. I doubt you have anything to say I want to hear either so I suggest you leave. Goodbye."

"Lady Genevieve said it's time to go, friend," Mira said. "Either you leave now, or we throw you out of here on your ear."

He stood up slowly. "You should be nicer to me love. I could be a lot of help to you, and believe me you're going to need help."

"Are you threatening me, Gregor?"

"Oh, no love," he said. "That isn't a threat, just a prediction. Believe me when I say your fancy war hero won't be able to save you."

Genevieve laughed in his face. "Anything you can do, Gideon can do a thousand times better," she sneered. "Goodbye, Gregor. Don't let the door hit you on your way out."

"See you around, love," he said as he sauntered out.

Genevieve made a growling sound.

"Hey, take it easy there boss," Marjorie said, "You're practically setting the place on fire with blue sparks."

Genevieve gave in to her worst instincts and sent a fat blue spark directly at Gregor's arrogant backside as he reached the door. She hit him dead center and he jumped and grabbed a buttock, glaring at her over his shoulder as he left.

Mira collapsed back into her chair in a fit of giggles. "Oh Goddess," she gasped, "I can't believe I just saw you do that!"

Marjorie was laughing too and she slapped the table so hard her cup of Cafka jumped, nearly spilling onto the table before she caught it. "I sure wish I could do that," she choked out. "I can see the aura, but I can't make it work for me that way."

"He's a bad man," pronounced Ceridwen with the absolute certainty of a nine-year-old.

"Yes," Genevieve agreed, "but I

shouldn't have done that, girls. In a fight, the woman who loses her temper always loses the battle. But it sure felt good."

"I wonder what he meant by us needing his help?" Mira speculated.

"Probably just hot air," Marjorie snorted.

Gideon was going to have a fit, Genevieve reflected. Gregor following her around would just confirm his suspicions about Gregor's motives. After last night, she had begun to realize just how possessive Gideon was. Was it too soon to hope his reaction meant he was beginning to love her, she wondered?

However, when they arrived back at Glass Manor and found Gideon waiting impatiently for her, it wasn't to talk about Gregor's misdeeds. An urgent message had been received from the Clan Patrol at Horned Cove, the bay on the far side of Veiled Isle.

"Veiled Isle, isn't that where Zack and Katherine went?" he asked.

"Yes, it is. What happened?"

He stuck the recording crystal into the player. The voice that came through was calm, but a little breathless. "Clarissa from Horned Cove Clan Patrol here. We just received an emergency message from the lookout at Karnelon Station. They say that they were unable to reach either Veiled Lodge or Glass Castle because they have only short-range communications available for some reason. They're under attack from a group of Wilders who crossed over from Neosicily Isle and landed in Stranger's Cove yesterday. These Wilders have some long-range plasma rifles. They appear to be attempting to move along the coast towards Hidden Valley. Clarissa Out."

Genevieve frowned. "They will have started Round Up on the Isle. Have you tried to get through to the Lodge yet?"

He shook his head. "I waited for you. I didn't know if you would want me to send additional manpower or not. I don't think there's any real hurry. From looking at a map of the Isle, it looks like several days before the Wilders would be able to reach the Valley."

"Veiled Isle is our second biggest settlement. Usually they have enough fighters to be able to handle these types of raids. Don't send additional manpower unless they ask for it. However, let's message them now so they are aware of the Wilder's movements."

Although it was late afternoon in Port Recovery, it was early morning at the Isle. Since Katherine had put the message on broadcast, Gideon and Genevieve were able to see the assembled wagons and Clansmen as well.

"Wow," he said when they had signed off. "Are we going to do that on Glass Isle too?"

Genevieve laughed. "No, we don't do Round Up. On Glass Isle, we mostly have Individual farms, factories, crystal mines and other stuff. Glass is more oriented towards trade with the Independent Fishing Fleets, other clans or the Free Trade Spacers Union than Veiled is. Veiled was settled by farmers and ranchers whose main exports are plants for cosmetics and medicines or animals for food or clothing. They do have a small harbor at Hooded Beach Cove that handles a few ships and another at Horned Cove. Corrine was always talking about developing some type of tourist industry but that was before the war started."

"I can understand the reasoning behind rounding up animals for culling before the swarms start, but I can see an increased need for security with so many people tied up with it."

Genevieve shrugged. "Well, they do have some advantages we don't on Glass. The Lodge is built over the top of an enormous underground cavern with a warm water lake, and there is Blue Talon Canyon that they use as an additional shelter. Veiled pretty much shuts down most of its outdoor activities during the season. We don't have the luxury of doing that on Glass Isle."

"No huge underground Cavern?" he inquired.

"No cavern. The port stays in business, so that means the town does as well. We do get a bigger influx of Independent Fishers and ships associated with other clans sheltering from the storms, and the crews don't always get along. The harbor is supposed to be neutral territory, but—"

"Tempers can get out of hand in

that situation," he agreed ruefully.

When Gideon came up to their room that evening he found Genevieve already dressed for bed. She was sitting cross-legged against the headboard making notes on her port-pad. He sat down on the side of the bed and began taking off his shoes.

"I just read the security report from this afternoon," he said. "Why didn't you tell me when you came in that Gregor followed you on your shopping trip? What did he want?"

She looked up from her tablet frowning. "With the news from Veiled Isle, I forgot about him," she admitted. "Other than making a nuisance of himself, I'm not sure what he wanted. He followed us into the Cafka shop, made a few snarky remarks about both of us. Said I was going to need help but he didn't say for what. It almost looked as if he just wanted to be seen talking to me. "He left when I told him to go. Of course, Mira did threaten to toss him out on his ear."

"Was he trying restart your relationship, or just to intimidate you?"

She coughed. "Well, if that's what he wanted I'm pretty sure he figured out neither one was going to happen."

He glanced sideways at her. "Really?"

"Yes, really," she said, poking him with her finger. 'And you know why too—I'm sure you heard all about it along with everyone else when we got back. Marjorie and Mira thought it was hilarious. I'm positive they couldn't keep the story to themselves. I'd be surprised it hasn't traveled back to Glass Isle by now."

"Well, I heard about the incident, but I'm not exactly sure what it was you did."

She made a face. "I hit him in the butt with a fat spark when he left. It was a really juvenile thing to do." She sighed. "I intended to start out my new career as a mother by setting an example of how to behave in public, and then the first time I take our new daughters for an outing, they have to see me do something a child would do," she added mournfully.

He just looked at her, obviously waiting for more of an explanation, so she obliged. "Okay, you remember the other night when we got attacked and I had that sparkly aura?"

"Uh-huh, I recall it bit me a little when I tried to touch it."

"Well, all those tiny sparks can be coalesced into what we call a fat spark that can be aimed at things. A fat spark packs a much bigger wallop than all those small ones."

"And you hit him in the backside with one? I wish I could have seen that," he said wistfully.

She looked up at him sharply. His green eyes were brimming with mischief and he was trying very hard not to laugh.

Finally, she gave in and laughed with him.

Messy Situations

AS SHE HAD foretold, the tale of her encounter with the Grand Duke of Ivanov had beaten them back to Glass Castle. Genevieve's actions received a mixed reception depending on who was talking about it. The new clan members, fresh from the interplanetary war were wholly in support of a physical response to an implied threat, as were many of the clan. Others, such as her assistant Mary McGregor, a holdover from Genevieve's mothers reign, thought she had made a serious political goof.

Hardly had Genevieve and her new family stepped through the

Castle door when Mary had cornered her to express disapproval. With all the assurance of an old and valued retainer, she demanded, "What do you have to say for yourself young lady? I can't believe you did something that childish. You can't go around sparking the Grand Duke of Ivanov in the rear—"

To everyone's surprise, Ceridwen marched up to Mary and said, "You leave her alone! He was a bad man!"

Checked in mid-flight, Mary glanced down at her. "And just who might you be, young Miss?"

Genevieve put a hand on Ceridwen's shoulder. "Mary, this Ceridwen and Bronwen Huron, my new daughters. Please make them welcome."

"Oh, yes, I heard about that. Welcome, Mi'Ladies to Glass Castle. I hope you will be happy here. Now Milady—"

She was interrupted a second time. Gideon came forward, placing a hand on Genevieve's shoulder in much the same way as she had with Ceridwen. "Mary," he said mildly. "The Laird had the right idea. Gregor Ivanov was attempting to intimidate her and thus Clan O'Teague. An answer needed to be made and she made it."

Genevieve looked at them both in bemusement. Not since she had taken the office of Laird at the tender age of seventeen had anyone offered her such whole-hearted support. A little spot she hadn't known was cold began to warm inside her.

"But he's the Grand Duke!" Mary wailed.

"I doubt the Tsarina sanctioned him following me around, Mary," Genevieve said firmly. "And while I value input from all the clan, I believe that subject is closed. Now, it was a long trip, and I'm tired. I want to get my new daughters settled in their rooms, eat dinner with my family and go to bed. Tomorrow will be soon enough to deal with anything Drusilla didn't handle in my absence."

The first of the swarms were seen off the coast the next day and could be expected to arrive within the week. That morning at a family breakfast that included Drusilla, Lucas and Jayla, Genevieve outlined the plan for handling damages from the swarming bugs.

"The first swarm is usually made up of very tiny insects," she explained. "While they are annoying, life pretty much goes on as usual. Of course, we will have to deal with the results of a few people or animals causing damage or hurting themselves because they panic. Gideon there are trained crews already set up for rescues in those cases. The swarms of larger bugs will begin arriving in increasing numbers about ten days after the first swarm and are more of a problem."

"How much time between swarms?" asked Lucas.

"Sometimes a couple of days, sometimes only a few hours,"

Drusilla answered. "The Dragon Talkers are kept busy in relays pushing the bigger insects to detour around as much of the harbor and town as we can. Fortunately, most of the actual Dragons will be hibernating during the next three months, otherwise we'd have to deal with them as well." She looked at Lucas thoughtfully. "You were a big help on the way out here as an Anchor Talker. However, since you haven't had the training, it would be better if you work as a part of my team since we don't know yet if you can connect with anyone except me."

"When this is over, I think Lucas should take the training," Genevieve suggested. "Providing that it's okay with you and Gideon, Lucas?"

He exchanged glances with Gideon. "Well, I am planning to specialize in security, but I think an additional skill wouldn't hurt. What do you think Gideon?"

Gideon nodded. "Yes, I think so. I've had complaints that Clan Patrol has had to wait for a Talker to come to them and move Dragons off rescues and crime scenes before they could go in. I was going to suggest that more of our security people take the training as well."

Genevieve looked at Drusilla. "As Chief Talker for the Clan, perhaps you could start the ball rolling with the Guild to arrange that."

Drusilla nodded agreeably. "I'll do that today."

"Chief?" asked Lucas. "Does that mean you're boss of the Clan

Dragon Talkers?"

"Yes, it does," Drusilla retorted. "So, once you get certified, it means you have to take orders from me."

"We want to help too," Ceridwen announced.

Genevieve smiled down at her. "Of course. I'll expect the two of you to stay inside the castle during the swarms or storms, but we will be getting a lot of displaced people sheltering here during that time and they will have children and pets with them. I was hoping that you and Bronwen could help out in making them welcome and entertaining them."

She looked thoughtfully at Jayla. "Jayla, Drusilla and I will be assisting on rescue teams a lot of the time, and the Clan will expect a member of the Laird's family to be in control of making sure that food, clothing and places to sleep is available for the refugees who will come in while we are busy. Would you be willing to be in charge of that?"

Jayla spilled her Cafka. "Me?" she squeaked in astonishment, staring at Genevieve with a mixture of pride and fear. This was the biggest thing that had ever happened to her. No one had ever offered her the responsibility of doing anything before. She had been more used to being regarded as a liability rather than an asset. "I—well, I guess so, but I don't know—"

Genevieve smiled at her. "Thank you. You can have Mary to assist you. She knows what has been done in the past and she can tell you who to assign to perform the actual work, but you will have to give the necessary orders."

Jayla gulped. "Okay."

"Don't worry if you don't get everything exactly right at first," Drusilla encouraged her. "Everyone will know it's a learning curve and cut you some slack. Just don't be afraid to ask questions."

The dining room was starting to clear out as guests and people who lived in the castle left for the day's duties. When Mary came over, Genevieve asked her to take Jayla around and introduce her to the housekeepers, cooks and the barn boss so she could get familiar with their plans for handling the influx of refugees who would soon be arriving.

"I have a meeting with the Clan Patrol this morning," Gideon told Genevieve as he kissed her goodbye. "I'll keep you updated on anything we need to handle."

Drusilla stopped Lucas as he started to follow Gideon. "Nope, you're with me this morning. We have a meeting with the Talkers to attend," she informed him.

When she dropped off Bronwen at the Day Nursery, Genevieve informed Jermaine who was supervisor that morning that both girls would be serving as hostess to the children of the refugees, Bronwen for the younger set, and Ceridwen for the school agers. Wanda Loris, the Castle's education coordinator, seemed pleased and agreed to help Ceridwen integrate any new students that might arrive.

As they fastened the mesh from their hats to their clothes, Gideon and Lucas now saw the virtue of the netting Katherine had insisted be added to their Vensoog attire. Without them, the tiny flying, biting gnats that first arrived would have made it impossible to work outside. The gnats were fast as they moved through an area, swarming over anything they met in a smothering cloud. Genevieve had been right, Gideon thought, the harbor and city conducted business as usual despite the gnats' interference. Entrances to buildings or vessels made humming sounds when entered, leaving piles of dead bugs to be periodically swept away.

While the nets provided protection from the first of the swarms, they weren't much help against the larger insects that arrived a few days later. The bigger flying pests were just as fast as the gnats and hit anything in their path with the force of small hailstones. This sometimes caused small ships to capsize or other transports to run into buildings because the driver's vision was impaired.

During this time, only two sets of refugees appeared and only one of them required shelter. The first refuges belonged to an Independent Fisher called Private Enterprise, which had capsized just before it reached the shelter of the harbor. Times had been hard, the Captain told Gideon and they had been attempting to get a bigger catch by taking advantage of the schools of fish coming to the surface to feed on the swarms. Unfortunately, an overlarge Sea Dragon attempting the same thing had surfaced too close to their ship, and the wave it produced had caused the ship to roll over. Private Enterprise was now upside down and sinking slowly to the ocean floor. The ship had gone down close enough to the Port for a rescue team to be dispatched to retrieve the hapless sailors, and Gideon had accompanied them 'because he needed the experience of a sea rescue to learn how it was done', he informed Genevieve.

Observing the sparkle in his green eyes when he said this, Genevieve had severe doubts that gaining experience was his only reason for going. No doubt the experience would be valuable to him, but she would have bet money he was expecting to enjoy it.

Since the crew of Private Enterprise were now broke and had no money for food or rooms, the Captain accepted the Laird's offer of shelter for herself and her crew, intending to make connections with some of the other Independents taking shelter in the crowded harbor.

Their arrival provided Jayla, Ceridwen and Bronwen some small experiences in dealing with the issues they might face during the storms. Within two days however, everyone had bigger problems to deal with; a swarm of large burrowing insects managed to dig under the dome housing the city power plant. While the bugs found nothing to eat in the dome, they left a hardening film of manure coating the fuel crystals. The covering of filth blocked the large Azorite crystals from emitting the power rays that ran most of the city utilities causing a citywide power outage. The plant had quickly shut everything down before an overload could occur, but the muck left by the bugs set hard and required several days of acid applications to remove.

Many of the larger houses and buildings including Glass Castle had independent generators but the fuel crystals used to operate them would only last a few days before needing to recharge. Genevieve had informed Jayla she was opening the Castle's doors to anyone who needed meals or a place to sleep while the damage was being repaired.

Then suddenly everything was quiet and still for about twenty-four hours. Glass City caught its breath and stepped up preparations for the coming storms. They heard the first storm before it arrived; a steadily increasing roar as first the wind and then the rain drew near, along with a tidal surge that raised the water level in the harbor. The Patrol command center got its first call for help about a half hour after the tide surged. The wind had knocked over a large rainbow hardwood tree and damaged one of the domes near the wharf. As a result, tidal surges were flooding the ground floor of the warehouse. Gideon headed out with the emergency repair team to assess the damage.

He was both proud and amused to find Jayla firmly handing out earmuffs to anyone leaving the castle, and fielding requests from housekeeping at the same time. "Annie was supposed to do this," she explained, "but she fell and broke her ankle so she's in the infirmary this morning."

"So, the boss is filling in, huh?" he asked. "Good job, kid."

Jayla blushed to the roots of her hair at his praise. "Thanks," she said in surprise.

The girl acted as if no one had ever told her she was doing a good job before. What had David and

Celia been thinking of he wondered, for the child to be so shocked at a few words of praise?

He found Genevieve at the scene discussing, if that term could be applied to an exchange conducted by both parties screaming to be heard over the roar of the wind, what kind of stopgap repairs could be done to prevent further damage during the interim while the storms passed.

"I'm ruined!" the man howled.

"Nonsense," she said briskly. "Put up a temporary wall to seal off the rest of the building. You can hire plenty of those idle Fishers in the harbor for that. The Clan will supply building materials at cost. Everything here that could be irreparably damaged by water will have to be moved to the upper floors of course, and mind you, the key word here is 'irreparably', so don't attempt to put everything in this warehouse up there Edwards, or there'll be another accident when the floor collapses. You were told last year to remove that tree because it was in danger of falling over in a high wind."

"It was such a beautiful tree," the man lamented.

"Yes, and think what beautiful things can be made from it. "That tree will bring you a good price as furniture wood," she retorted.

Gideon's people had finished going through the building and rescued the two workers trapped under the tree. Fortunately, neither had been injured beyond bruising.

"Why can't they build the wall," demanded Edwards, indicating Gideon's rescue workers.

Gideon stared down at him. "Members of the Patrol are needed for emergencies just now. I'm not tying up valuable personnel to do construction projects for you. The O'Teague just gave you a solution. I suggest you use it." He turned to Genevieve, "None injured worth taking to an infirmary. We're heading back. I'll see you there."

Sirens began to wail over the noise of the wind. "What is that?" he asked her.

"The siren means the wind speed is increasing to a dangerous level and to take shelter. You need to recall everyone still out and tell them to return to base or get under cover until the storm eye passes over us."

"You too," he said firmly.

She nodded. "You can give me a ride back to the Castle."

Genevieve was so busy over the next weeks she barely noticed the difference from one day to the next. She was tired and to make matters worse, she wasn't eating because practically everything she tried didn't taste good to her or it smelled funny. Not wanting to hurt Jayla's feelings (the girl had been doing a wonderful job keeping things running) she had finally asked Drusilla privately to check the food stores for contamination.

Her sister just looked at her. "It isn't the food," she was told. "It's you. Let me guess, everything smells bad and tastes worse?"

"How did you know that?"

"It's a part of my talent, remember? When was the last time you had your monthly?"

Genevieve thought back. "I think it was before the swarms came. I don't remember having it last month."

"Uh-huh. I think a trip to the infirmary might be in order, Sis. You are a married woman now, and it's a possibility."

"Oh," Genevieve said rather blankly. "Sure, I'll go in as soon as I have the time."

Drusilla made a rude noise. "Maybe you should make the time."

Genevieve's com chimed. It was Gideon. "Genevieve, we need as many volunteers as you can muster out on the east side of the harbor. We have a mudslide here that's about to skid a couple of homes into the bay."

"Got it. Keep everyone as safe as you can. You too," she replied, switching her com to the Castle broadcasting system. "Attention please, this is the O'Teague. We have a stage two emergency out at East Harbor. All emergency teams please assemble in the transport center. It's a mudslide so we'll need first aid kits, shovels, ropes and floatation devices. Mark: ten minutes until departure."

On the way to collect her own gear, she heard Jayla asking Mary how many people lived on the east side so they could decide how many beds to prepare. The girl had certainly handled the responsibility dumped on her well, Genevieve reflected. She was doing an excellent job.

Genevieve stopped and gave her a hug. "Thanks, Hon," she said to Jayla. "I knew you were up to handling this. I just want you to know, this season has gone so much smoother with you taking some of the load. Mary you've been a blessing this season as well."

The land on the east side of the harbor consisted of cliffs made of soft dirt providing no real anchorage for buildings. The ground tended to soften and slide toward the harbor if it became saturated as it was now.

Genevieve had recommended against building there, but some enterprising clan members had insisted on doing so contrary to her advice. Additionally, the waters on this side of the bay were very shallow with rocky outcrops jutting out making boating very dangerous.

It looked as though some of the cliffs had collapsed and slid into the harbor. Two of the house domes were already halfway in the water. Remarkably, their floors were still attached so the domes looked like half drowned eggs. The wharf was gone and the ships anchored closest to it had been pushed out in the center of the bay. The wind wasn't at full strength, but it was making the shuttles difficult to keep in the air while rescuers went down safety lines to pull up stranded refugees.

She found Gideon and several members of his team waist deep in the moving mud as they tried to keep a couple of people from sinking.

Looking out she spotted several more people trapped in the mud and water. Genevieve leaned out from the open door of the first of the three air sleds she had brought and tossed out three lines attached to rescue harnesses. Gideon took the line intended for him and attached it to a woman with the child she was holding, signaling for them to be pulled up.

Genevieve swore and jumped down beside him, holding onto a second harness. "You idiot!" she cried. "Are you trying to get yourself drowned in mud? Put this on! If you go under you can't help anyone else."

He grinned at her out of a mud-covered face. "You're no better," he retorted, doing as she asked. "You aren't big enough to be fishing around in this muck. You just want to join in the fun."

"We need to have a serious discussion about what you think of as fun," she said. As she spoke, she spotted a couple trying to climb out of the harbor onto one of the rocks in the shallow waters and signaled the sled to move towards them.

When it was over and she was back at the castle wrapped in a warmed blanket, sipping the hot Cafka Jayla had handed to her she looked over at Gideon. "We were lucky today," she said quietly.

"Yes," he agreed, sipping on his own cup. "I sure expected to lose a couple of clansmen in that mudslide. As it was we got by with a broken arm and some property damage."

She made a face at him. "Yes, well maybe the next time the town council will listen when I recommend not building somewhere."

He looked at her curiously. "Could you have prevented it?"

She sighed. "Not really. It's a pretty independent bunch we have here. The land around the harbor was ceded to the town by my Great Grandmother and the town council decides on civil matters like the sale of property it has title to. As Laird, I can advise them about stuff and I although I can overrule them in cases of danger to the clan, I usually prefer not to do so unless I absolutely must."

"It's impossible to lead without the consent of those being led," he misquoted.

"Yes," she agreed.

He turned his head to watch his niece handing out more cups of hot Cafka to the survivors. "I confess, I was doubtful when you handed off that job to her, but she's done really well hasn't she?"

"She has, and I told her so this morning. I don't mean to cast aspersions on your brother and his wife, but—"

"I know," he said. "It occurred to me earlier too when I told her what a great job she was doing. The poor kid was shocked. Are we going to let her go back to hiding in her room when this is over?"

"Well, unless you have some

objection, I would like her to continue doing what she is now. The responsibility has done more to make her feel a part of things than anything else we've tried. I think I'll tell her I need her to keep handling this stuff so I can have a little time off occasionally." She yawned, "You'll be glad to know that Patrice reports that this was the last storm. All we have left is cleaning up after it."

She rose and set her cup on an empty tray with several others. "I don't know about you, but after this last one, I want a bath and then bed. Girls!" she called to Ceridwen and Bronwen, "say goodnight to your new friends. Its bedtime."

She gave Jayla a peck on the cheek. "Good night, sweetie. Don't work too hard tonight. Tomorrow we have to start cleaning up after all of this."

Gideon ruffled her hair as he passed. "I'm proud of you kid," he said as he followed his wife to the stairs.

Now that the storms had passed, Genevieve and Gideon had intended to spend the next day organizing repairs to be done. The call from Corrine reporting the attack at the Lodge and its results came in just as they were about to leave for breakfast.

"How badly was Katherine hurt?" Genevieve demanded.

"Stabbed in the leg," Corrine said briefly. "She lost a lot of blood, but Zack did a field dressing and she'll be fine. Cora is making her stay in bed for a few days though. We lost two of our own."

"The dead woman was DeMedici?" Genevieve asked.

"Yes," responded Corrine. "She was the one who attacked little Juliette on the Dancing Gryphon. I know she was one of Lewiston's lieutenants."

"Did Lewiston plan this?" Gideon asked.

It was Vernal who answered. "Well, that's a case of what we know versus what we can prove, I'm afraid. None of the ex-soldiers we captured who are willing to testify heard him give her the orders."

"We have another problem as well," Corrine said. "At least six of the men we captured surrendered when they realized it was Zack they were attacking. He had saved their lives in some action in the war. He thinks Lewiston won't take them back, or if he does, he might kill them out of hand. He and Katherine offered to allow them to switch clans if that turns out to be the case."

Ceridwen tugged on Genevieve's hand. "Aren't we going to eat?"

"Gideon and I have to finish this com, but why don't the pair of you go down and get started. We'll be down as soon as we can."

"Really?" Bronwen asked excitedly.

"Yes, really. I'm sure that both of you are big enough to go down to the cafeteria and ask for what you want at breakfast. Make more than one trip to the table if necessary, Ceridwen."

"Okay, C'mon let's go Bron," she said racing for the door.

Corrine took up the story again when Genevieve returned to the com. "We have a couple of Independent Fishers who took shelter here. I think they'd like to become affiliated or at least receive favored status, so I was planning on sending them over to you to negotiate terms."

"You mean you haven't done so already?" Genevieve asked.

"Don't get sassy girl. I didn't want to step on any toes," Corrine retorted.

"Zack and I'll be sending you over the soldiers along with Lister's and the other bodies as well as the prisoners," interrupted Vernal before things were sidetracked.

Genevieve nodded. "They would have to swear fealty to O'Teague in any case if DeMedici won't have them back. I can contact LaDoña about them when I inform her we will be returning Lister's body."

"You said six surrendered without a fight," Gideon inquired. "What about the others?"

"Five dead and seven Prisoners. They aren't talking much. We'll be sending them along too."

Gideon turned to Genevieve. "Do you want to handle this as case of lawbreaking or send them home as legitimate prisoners?"

"Politically, speaking, since they claim to be DeMedici, that clan has the right to speak for them at any judgement hearing. If they won't say that they were under orders, it's going to depend on what I find out when I contact LaDoña. Yes, send them here as well as the men who might become O'Teague."

The communication between O'Teague and DeMedici was short and unpleasant.

One of Lewiston's people answered the com. When Genevieve asked to be put through to LaDoña, Lewiston himself came on the vid.

"Can I help you?" he asked his voice just on the edge of insolent.

Genevieve frowned at him. "Please put me through to LaDoña," she said. "What I need to say is best transmitted Clan Head to Clan Head."

"Sorry, LaDoña is busy with other items. Give me the message."

"Very well," she said her voice

chilly. "Please inform LaDoña that due to what (now) I am assuming was an unauthorized raid on O'Teague lands, arrangements need to be made to return several bodies and prisoners to DeMedici. I will await her communication."

Lewiston's mouth pinched tight. "I want to know who was killed," he said.

"Certainly," Genevieve replied as if bored and transmitted the list. "You did not ask, but please inform LaDoña that the raid was unsuccessful. I am sure LaDoña will be relieved to know my people suffered only two fatalities. I will be returning the prisoners and bodies of the raiders to the Security offices in Port Recovery on the tenth of this month."

"Thank you," Lewiston bit out.

Genevieve cut the communication and sat thoughtfully tapping her finger on her desk.

"You didn't bring up Thompson and his crew," Gideon who had been quietly watching her, said.

"No, and I don't intend to, not with him."

"I'm unfamiliar with how the other clans work," he said. "Would LaDoña really have just turned over so much to him that she wouldn't take calls from other clan heads?"

"No," Genevieve responded, "She would not. LaDoña is one very tough, feisty old woman. I can't see her doing that and even if she did, it wouldn't be to a newcomer. She would have turned things over to her First Daughter."

"That's Doña Sabina?"

"Yes."

Gideon sighed. "Doña Sabina, to whom he is probably giving Submit to control her. This is likely to get ugly, Genevieve."

"I know," she said, holding out her hand to him. "We can handle it."

He raised her hand to his mouth and kissed it.

"Yes, we will handle it," he replied.

Accusations

GIDEON WAS certainly doing everything he could to learn about all aspects of his position as Head of Security for the O'Teague clan, Genevieve reflected yawning. That morning though, she could have wished his devotion to duty hadn't included rising at such an unholy hour. He and Lucas were joining the Glass Harbor Patrol for a pre-dawn excursion that apparently included inspecting a couple of fishing boats leaving after the storms. The three boats were suspected of receiving items looted from some of the damaged warehouses. She kissed him goodbye at the door of their room and stumbled back into bed. When Gorla woke her demanding to be fed, it was still early, but at least the sun was peeking over the horizon.

As she stood up, a wave of vertigo hit her and she flopped back down on the bed. Gorla hopped up onto her shoulder and sniffed her face worriedly.

"I'm okay," she reassured the little creature. "Just give me a minute."

It was several minutes before she felt steady enough to get up and dress. When she checked on Ceridwen and Bronwen, she found them up and dressing, so she took them along for breakfast in the main hall. Not that many inhabitants of the castle were stirring this early;

she was able to enjoy her first cup of Cafka without being besieged by clansmen wanting her to solve a storm damage problem for them. The quiet chatter of the girls as they fed the Quirkas and themselves was soothing. This morning Genevieve even managed a second cup of Cafka with her breakfast before anyone discovered she was present.

She watched Mary, her assistant, approach with a formally dressed, tired looking man in the uniform of the Parliamentary Security Council.

"Good Morning, Milady," Mary said formally, "this gentleman has a message from the Council that he says is urgent."

Genevieve's eyebrows rose. "Life and Death urgent as in we're being attacked right this moment, or as in it needs to be looked at as soon as possible?" she asked.

"As soon as possible, Milady," the messenger said bowing.

"Very well," she responded. "Mary, get him some breakfast and then both of you report to my office when he's finished. Come along, girls" she addressed her adopted daughters, "since I see you've finished eating, lets clean up our area and then we will go back upstairs to wash up."

After turning the two girls over to Jermaine, the governess she had employed to make sure Ceridwen attended her lessons and Bronwen arrived at the Castle Day nursery, Genevieve treated herself to another cup of Cafka before she made her first appearance in her office.

Although there already were several petitioners in the reception area waiting for her attention, she motioned the messenger to follow her inside the office and shut the door.

He handed her a crystal message cube and said, "The Planetary Security Council requests your presence and that of your sister, Lady Katherine on the fifth of next month to answer charges regarding the death of Dame Darla Lister."

"Charges," she repeated. "What charges?"

The messenger looked uncomfortable. "I believe Clan DeMedici intends to prefer charges of wrongful death, Milady. I understand the details are in the cube."

Genevieve nodded. "Very well." She held out her hand, "If you will give me the acknowledgement, I will sign it now."

Silently, he held out another cube and she placed her hand on it, repeating her name and title.

The messenger bowed. "If you will excuse me, I need to be on my way to Veiled Isle to present Lady Katherine with the message as well."

"See that he has transportation, please Mary," Genevieve said, "and tell my first appointment there will be a slight delay." She waited until they had gone before she listened to the information on the cube, and then contacted Gideon asking him to come to her office as soon as he could. Her next communication was to her sister.

"He's done what?" demanded Katherine.

"There's going to be a formal hearing in Port Recovery next month," Genevieve repeated. "The messenger just left to come to you so you should have a copy of the charges by this evening. I'm contacting Jess Byrdon to handle our defense. I'm going to ask her come here and debrief us. I'll let you know as soon as I have a date for her arrival. In the meantime, I suggest you consider who you want her to call as witnesses."

Katherine made a rude noise and closed the communication.

"Problem?" Gideon inquired as he entered.

"It never rains, but it pours,"

Genevieve answered. "Lewiston's managed to push through a hearing before the Security Council into the death of Darla Lister. Here," she tapped the cube, "you'd better listen to it yourself."

She put her elbows on the desk and thrust her hands into her hair. "I think I'm getting a headache with Lewiston's name on it."

He patted her shoulder as he sat down beside her. "Messenger already gone?"

She snorted. "He took off like a scalded Quirka just as soon as he dropped his bomb. He's headed Katherine's way. I just told her, and from her reaction, I only hope she doesn't try to skin him for bearing bad news."

He listened to the charges in

frowning silence as related on the cube. "How seriously do we need to take this?"

"Well, it could get pretty nasty," Genevieve admitted. "Lister was from DeMedici so this hearing is liable to be a political hot potato. However, our clan lawyer, Jess Byrdon can be meaner than a bug swarm in the courtroom and she does love a good fight."

He stood up and started massaging her shoulders. "Okay. I need to get on the same page with you though. If the decision goes against us do we fight or turn Katherine over to them?"

Genevieve leaned back against him gratefully. "We aren't turning Katherine over on a murder charge because she eliminated a threat to one of her children."

"If we lose are we going to have to fight all the clans or just DeMedici?"

Genevieve shrugged. "We probably won't have to fight anyone if we can get Katherine back to O'Teague lands safely."

"Oh?" he asked. "Won't they demand we return her to them for sentencing?"

"Oh, there will be a request for it, but the Council won't be able to enforce it. You see, the Security Council's mandate is to coordinate any planetary defense necessary and enforce the law inside Port Recovery and along the water channels. Inside a clan's territory, they don't have any clout unless a clan grants it to them. That kind of authority is usually decided on a case-by-case basis at a Clan hearing. If a Clan's decision is different from the verdict reached during a Security Council trial, we aren't obligated to honor their ruling and they can't enforce it. They can't compel a clan to comply with judgement outside Port Recovery City or the channels. The founders made sure of that because the Security Council doesn't have a standing army. The Founders didn't want that much power concentrated into a central authority. During a planetary threat, each Clan's Security force must agree to work together and I don't see that happening in this case. Lister's death wouldn't be cause enough to overcome any long-standing bad feelings. There are too many past conflicts and current issues between the clans for any coordinated effort to work well." She grimaced. "You should have seen how hard it was just to get everyone to cooperate when the Karaminetes attacked us."

"Once we are back on our own lands will they send a bounty hunter after Katherine?"

She looked at him in horror. "I never thought of that. I doubt if the Council would sanction it, but I suppose DeMedici might do it on a private basis."

"Well, that's clear enough," he said calmly. "I have about a month to prepare a plan to get us all out of the capital in a hurry if we have to. We'll deal with the issue of a bounty hunter if and when it happens." He smiled down at her. "This is what Zack and I were trained for, you know. We can handle this."

"I know," she said returning his smile through watering eyes. "You have no idea how glad I am you're here." Angrily, she dashed a hand over her eyes. "Sorry, I didn't mean to flood on you. I don't know why I've been so weepy, lately."

The Clan lawyer, Jess Byrdon, was a tiny woman whose appearance was wildly at variance with her personality. Most people looking at her would have been fooled into seeing nothing but the big blue eyes and mop of golden curls. A mistake few made a second time. She listened to Katherine and Zack's story in silence and then outlined a list of people she needed to prepare as witnesses.

"Humm, Linda Delgado out of Rodriguez is up for Accuser this session. She'll be a tough opponent, even if her case is a load of crap." she remarked.

She considered for a moment, tapping her fingers on the arm of her chair. Then she nodded decisively. "You," she pointed a finger at Katherine, "I want to look like everyone's mother in court. Pull your hair back, loosen the clothes, and no makeup."

Jess turned to Juliette. "Her, I want to look as cute as a button. Put her hair in pigtails and put some ribbons in it. It would help if she carried a doll into the courtroom. Do you have a doll?" she asked Juliette.

"Uh, no, I don't think—"

"Get her one!" she snapped at Katherine, "the bigger and more conspicuous the better."

She turned to Zack, "Will those fighters you adopted into the clan testify about Lister's actions?"

"Yes, sure."

"Get them here. What about the fishers she attacked?"

"I'll contact them," Katherine said. "I'm sure the captain won't mind testifying."

Jess nodded. "Good. I'll want everyone here at least a week before we need to be in the capital so I can debrief them."

She turned to Gideon. "I'll want all the witness, except Juliette of course, to travel separately and I want them guarded like Katherine's life depends on it, because it might."

"Are they in danger?" Genevieve asked, alarmed.

"I don't have a clue if they are or not, but I learned a long time ago not to take any chances. I'm going to want to see everyone in court every day. Children included."

"I thought we would leave the children here," began Genevieve.

"No, no, no. We can't afford to look weak in this. If we want the council to accept that Katherine acted to defend her child, then we need to act as if the victory is a forgone conclusion. Any questions? No? Okay, I'll be in my room studying up on case law."

"Whew!" Zack exclaimed after she left. "Can anyone say Hurricane Jess?" He looked over at Katherine. "I guess we better go out and buy three dolls. I sure hope she doesn't want the boys in short pants."

"Idiot!" Katherine laughed.

"Zack, why don't we give you a pass on the doll shopping?" Genevieve suggested. "I better go with Katherine because we're going to need two more dolls for Ceridwen and Bronwen as well. Katherine and I can take our girls so they can pick out dolls, and make it an all-girl shopping trip. That way you and Gideon will be free to work on the plan to get us out of the city."

"Why are we all acting as if Mom is going to be convicted?" Juliette asked sharply.

"None of us believe I will be," Katherine reassured her, "but it's always better to have contingency plans in place. I just had a delightful thought—I wonder what Jess will say when she learns Violet is going to bring Jelli into the courtroom with her."

"Who cares about what Jess will say? Just think what the bailiff is likely to say," Genevieve retorted.

When she and Katherine traveled to Port Recovery for the hearing, Genevieve had left Drusilla behind again as her deputy. Drusilla had stood in for her before and she had no doubt of her being able to handle the administrative part of being Laird. Despite this, she was a little worried about the raiders taking advantage of the absence of both Gideon and herself to attack the Isle. Drusilla had Lucas as security to back her up, she reminded herself, and if he needed help

Gideon had assigned an experienced master sergeant to help him. Corrine and Vernal were handling matters at Veiled Isle, O'Teague's next largest settlement. The fisher fleet captain had scorned an escort and sailed up the river to the port as soon as she had spoken to Jess Byrdon.

Both Zack and Gideon had elected to take the dangerous duty of escorting the other witnesses to Port Recovery using two other air shuttles, one of whom would serve as a decoy.

The family party arrived at Glass Manor just as dusk was falling. What would have taken two weeks by riverboat, had only taken one day using an air shuttle, but it had still been a noisy, tiring trip. They had traveled with an escort of ten of Gideon's best security, but although the Security team would have been quite capable of fighting off an attack had there been one, they had proved no help at all in dealing with tired, bored children and an air-sick Sand Dragon.

One piece of good news had been that Ceridwen and Violet who were both of an age appeared to be on the way to becoming fast friends. Unfortunately, this left Bronwen feeling left out and she showed a tendency to cling to Genevieve. While both Jermaine and Jayne had come with them to assist with the children during the court sessions, it still meant that the women had been outnumbered by children on the trip. At the last minute, Jayla had elected to come with them, but her gifts didn't include amusing children much younger than herself and she spent most of her time involved in a game on her handheld.

The security force at Glass Manor seemed to have doubled, Genevieve observed as she carried a sleepy Bronwen ashore. She handed the child over to Mira to take up to the manor and turned to watch Katherine and several of the security people attempting to persuade a reluctant Jelli to step off the shuttle and onto the dock. Jelli hadn't liked traveling on the shuttle, and she liked the difference between the rocking shuttle and the wooden landing dock even less. Jelli's skin plates, which ordinarily would have shown a healthy pigment reflecting

the color of her surroundings, were
a pale, sickly green. Now as big and
heavy as an Old Earth mastiff dog, it
was proving very awkward to simply
pick her up and shove her through
the narrow shuttle opening when
she didn't want to be moved.
Finally, to everyone's surprise, Violet
marched up to the door of the
shuttle and said firmly, "Jelli, you
stop this right now. Nothing is going
to happen to you except maybe
getting wet. Come out of there
now!"

There was an irritable snort, and
then the dragon simply did as she
was told. She was received with
praise by Violet, who cooed at her,
"There, you big silly, you're such a
brave girl. Come along now and
we'll get you something to eat to

replace what you chucked up. You're a growing girl and you have to keep up your strength."

One of the security people stepped forward. "Right this way, Lady Violet," she said. "We set you two up on the ground floor, and some dinner for Jelli is already waiting with a stasis cube to keep it fresh."

"Thank you," Violet said. "I'm sorry; I don't know your name."

"It's Andrea Lansing," she was told.

"Thank you, Andrea. Jelli isn't usually this grouchy, but she's hungry because she was airsick and threw up breakfast." Violet turned to her new friend. "C'mon Ceri," she said, "I'll show you how to feed a dragon."

ail Daley

After putting the children to bed, both Genevieve and Katherine sat up in their nightclothes, waiting for their menfolk to arrive with the other witnesses, whose arrival had been planned to happen using the cover of darkness.

Katherine handed her sister a cup of Cafka and settled in a chair opposite her in a corner of the common room, tucking the skirts of her robe around her curled up legs. Sooka settled in on her lap.

"Are you feeling, alright, sister?" Genevieve asked her, stroking Gorla.

Katherine smiled wryly back at her. "I'm fine; I'm a little worried about Juliette though. Something is bothering her."

Genevieve looked at her in

surprise. "The two of you seem so close. Surely she would tell you if something was really wrong."

"Well, I hope so, but Juliette is a very reserved child. It took her a long time to come to trust me. She tends to keep her own counsel and make her own plans and she's not above taking independent action without telling me first. I suppose that comes from being on her own for so long."

"I thought all the children had come from a child placement center," Genevieve said in surprise.

"They did but from things the kids have let drop I really doubt that Grouters was a traditional placement center," Katherine said dryly. "He seems to have used the children as some kind of information gathering crew, and I do know that he had ties to a child trafficking ring, because IPP busted it just after we removed our children. Sometimes it breaks my heart to think about what they might have had to do to survive there."

"That's awful," Genevieve said. "Gideon told me that Jayla's upbringing had been very different from the other children's but I hadn't realized just how different he meant."

The two women talked about inconsequential things, gradually falling silent as the day caught up with them. Genevieve was practically falling asleep in the chair when the men arrived, but she managed to wake up enough to direct the ex-soldiers to one of the dormitories for the night. The Captain of the Independent fishers had elected to stay on her boat, which was docked at Glass Manor's wharf.

Once she felt her husband's reassuring warmth beside her in bed, Genevieve went immediately to sleep.

Around three in the morning, six men landed on the beach and slipped along the spinney hedge surrounding the estate. The two guards on patrol at the edge of the property never felt the sharp stab of the tranquilizer darts that took them out. On their way to the Manor, the intruders took out four more guards the same way.

In the downstairs room allotted to Violet, Jelli lifted her head and sniffed the air coming in through the open screen door leading out to the garden. Her ears lifted, but since the men she heard didn't attempt to enter the room, she concluded they were part of the guards and relaxed.

Upstairs, the same comfortable conviction didn't occur to Gorla who had the seen the intruders' arrival from Genevieve's terrace. The Quirka chirped in Genevieve's ear and pulled her hair, attempting to wake her up. When Genevieve didn't stir, she turned her attention to Gideon, who was easier to rouse. He came abruptly awake to find Gorla nose to nose with him and patting his face with her tiny hands. Instead of the normal feelings of contentment or hunger he usually received from her, this time he felt a sense of urgency and alarm.

"What's the matter, girl?" he asked. Sitting up on the side of the bed, he listened to the sounds of the house. Although he heard nothing, his soldier's intuitive awareness of danger caused him to dress and belt on his sidearm. He shook Genevieve's shoulder.

"Wake up honey," he whispered.

"What?" fuzzily she opened her eyes and sat up. "Why are you dressed?"

"Gorla says there's something wrong," he said softly. "I'm going to wake up Zack and check it out. You'd better go down the hall and wait with the girls."

Not waiting to see if she obeyed him, he slipped out the door. He met Zack in the corridor.

"Sooka woke us," Zack said softly. "Katherine's gone to collect the children."

They were soon joined by Thompson and the others.

Gideon made a closed fist, the sign for quiet, and then opened his hand twice to show there were six intruders.

"What happened to the outside patrol?" Zack asked softly. Gideon nodded to show he understood.

The intruders seemed to know exactly where they were going. They ignored most of the permanent residents' quarters on the lower floor and headed up the stairs towards the guest quarters used by the Laird and her family. Before they could finish their silent assent, one of the invaders apparently decided to check out Violets room. This proved to be a big mistake, and he retreated hastily with a loud yelp after an equally loud warning snarl from Jelli. Recoiling, he collided with a nearby table, knocking over a glass flower vase, which shattered noisily when it hit the tiled floor.

The resulting racket caused doors to open downstairs and heads to poke out demanding to know what the ruckus was about. At this point, Gideon signaled Zack to turn on the house lights. The intruders' night vision gear caused them to be temporarily blinded by the bright lights. Yanking off their headsets, they took one look at the armed contingent waiting for them at the top of the stairs and attempted a fast escape the way they came in.

The remainder of Gideon's security patrol had been alerted by the noise and lights and rushed into the downstairs hallway and common room. The two groups ran smack into each other, and a loud, noisy fight erupted. Questions and instructions and were yelled out and ignored. Furniture was knocked over and tables broken. Unable to fire their weapons for fear of hitting their own men, Gideon, Zack and the rest of the men on the stairs rushed down to help subdue the intruders. They were soon joined by at least half of the household staff, which increased the noise and confusion threefold. In the doorway to Violets room Jelli bounced up and down emitting squeals of excitement, and was only prevented from joining the melee by her small mistress's orders.

Once the captured intruders had been put under lock and key, and his unconscious guards found and revived, Gideon went upstairs to look for Genevieve. He found her, Jayla and a very worried Jermaine in the younger girls' room. "I only turned my back for a moment, Milady," Jermaine said tearfully. "When I looked back they were gone."

"I expect they're hiding," Genevieve reassured her. "Bronwen? Ceridwen? It's safe to come out now girls." She waited patiently until the two girls crept out from under the bed, and then knelt holding out her arms. There was a brief hesitation, and then first

Bronwen and then Ceridwen ran to her, crying.

"It's alright," she soothed. "I've got you. Lord Gideon caught the intruders. There's nothing to be afraid of."

Ceridwen looked up at him. "Are they gone?"

Gideon knelt by Genevieve enfolding all of them in his arms. "I didn't run them off, hon. I caught them so I can find out why they came here. That way I can keep them from coming back and make sure my family is safe."

"Are we your family?" the child asked with heartrending simplicity.

"Yes," he replied, hugging them all before he helped Genevieve to her feet.

"We've had quite an exciting

night," Genevieve said. "Put on your night robes girls, and we'll all go down to the kitchen and make a hot drink to help us sleep."

The Trial

TRIALS IN Port Recovery were held in the City Hall, a wide, triple-dome affair originally used to house many of the immigrants before the clans had moved out to the nearby islands. It now served a variety of municipal purposes.

When the O'Teague party arrived at the City courthouse the next morning, the bailiff at the entrance wasn't happy to see Jelli. "See here," she protested, "you can't bring that thing in here."

Violet drew closer to Jelli, who curled her lip at the guard. Thanks to a recent growth spurt, Jelli was now as tall at the shoulders as her mistress's head and appeared quite intimidating. "She goes everywhere with me," Violet announced militantly.

As Genevieve swept up the stairs to confront the Bailiff, she motioned for Violet to go on into the courthouse. "That thing, as you call her, saved my niece's life. She has proven her worth and loyalty. Most certainly, she will stay with her. You are not, I trust expecting a nine-year old child to stay alone outside while her mother is on trial?"

The guard eyed the Laird O'Teague unhappily. Out of the corner of her eye, she could see Jelli's tail disappearing through the doors in Violet's wake. The situation had spiraled out of her control and she knew it. "That will be up to the judges Ma'am," she said, surrendering.

The court was presided over by a panel of three judges. Although they would make decisions in a body, one judge acted as spokesperson.

The trial dragged on for most of the morning, while Jess Byrdon and Linda Delgado battled it out between them.

The Accuser, Linda Delgado, was a tall, well-built woman with a mane of dark hair and bright red lip dye. Delgado had Major Lewiston as her final witness, testify as to Darla Lister's service record.

"Was she a good soldier?" she asked him.

"Exceptional," he replied. "I never had cause to place any disciplinary orders in her file."

"To your knowledge, what was her relationship with Zackery Jackson, prior to Lady Katherine's arrival on Fenris?"

"I believe it was romantic," he replied.

"Did that change?"

"Well, I think she said they had several dates afterwards, but they were keeping them quiet," he said.

"So, you think Lady Katherine killed her out of jealousy?"

"Yes, I do," he said.

Jess Brydon looked him over thoughtfully before she began her cross-examination.

"You say you never put any bad conduct marks in Lister's file, Don Tomas, but what about your own?"

He eyed her suspiciously. "I don't know what you mean."

"Well, isn't it a fact that you were investigated for your part in an attempted coup on Janus just before the war ended?"

"I was cleared of that," he said defensively.

"That isn't quite true, is it?" she said. "I believe the inquiry was dropped for lack of evidence because a couple of witnesses disappeared. Witnesses whose disappearance was linked to Darla Lister, isn't that true?"

"Your honors, I protest," Dame Delgado said. "This has nothing to do with the present inquiry."

"Your honors, I believe it does," Byrdon said. "It shows that this witness has a motive to lie about Darla Lister's reputation."

"We agree," the judges said. "The

witness will answer."

"Yes, but suspicion isn't proof," Lewiston said.

Jess leaned back against her table and crossed her arms. "Perhaps. Did you attend the Captain's Mast aboard the Dancing Gryphon?"

"Yes."

"And the reason for that Captain's Mast?"

He glared at her. "Darla was accused of locking a child into an unheated locker."

"And the name of that child?" she prompted.

Lewiston puffed out a breath. "Juliette Jones," he said curtly.

"Lady Katherine's adopted daughter?"

"Yes," he snapped.

"If she had not been found and released, Lady Juliette would have died of cold and starvation, wouldn't she?" Dame Byrdon said.

"It's possible," he admitted. "But Darla only wanted to teach the kid a lesson. She would have gone back and let her out."

"Really?" the Defender said. "Apparently, Lady Katherine had good reason to assume Lister bore Juliette some animosity."

Jess called the captain of the Independent Fishers as her first witness. The captain identified Darla Lister as the leader of the group who had attacked her ship and taken her crew prisoner. Leroy Thompson, the leader of the six soldiers who had surrendered to Zack identified Lister as the leader of the group. When it came time to question Zack, Braydon went directly to the heart of the Accusers claim that Katherine had killed Lister out of jealousy.

"Lord Zachery, some questions have been raised as to your relationship with Darla Lister, before and after you became engaged to Lady Katherine. Can you tell us about that relationship?"

Zack snorted. "Lister was a good-looking woman. Before I saw Katherine, we went out a couple of times."

"Was it romantic?" she asked him.

"I wouldn't, myself, call it a romance," he replied. "Just a couple of dates were all it was. Truthfully, she was kind of boring out of bed and she lost interest in any kind of relationship when she found I wasn't interested in making any private deals for military weapons."

"I wasn't aware that military personal were permitted to sell military weapons on the private market."

"We aren't," Zack replied. He let it lie there.

"And what happened when you met Lady Katherine?" Jess asked him.

He smiled directly at Katherine from the stand. "I got hit with a robo-tanker and went down for the last time. She is the smartest, kindest, most beautiful woman I have ever known."

"So you and Lister didn't have any dates once you'd met Katherine?"

"Well I sure didn't notice any," he retorted, and the audience laughed.

Dame Byrdon coughed. "Yes, well moving along, tell me about the Captain's Mast."

"Captain Heidelberg found Darla Lister guilty of attempting to hurt Juliette. The Captain locked her up in the brig for the remainder of the journey," Zack said flatly. "She tried to slap Juliette while she was testifying there too, but Katherine stopped her." He grinned remembering. "Knocked her right on her ass."

When it was her turn, the Accuser said, "I have no questions for this witness, your honors."

Katherine's testimony agreed with Zacks. She made no apology, for either her threat to Lister aboard the Dancing Gryphon, or later when she followed her into a tunnel to stop her going after Juliette.

"She pulled out her combat knife and jumped at me," Katherine said. "I had to pull my own to stop the blade coming at me. I didn't have an opportunity to pull my gun. During the fight, I was wounded in the leg and spent several days in the infirmary afterwards. I've been reliably informed I was very lucky she didn't kill me at the time; I'm certainly not the expert at close-in knife fighting that Lister was."

When asked point-blank if she had felt her daughter's life was in danger from Lister, she had answered, "Absolutely."

Juliette took her doll on the stand with her, causing a ripple of amusement from the audience as Jess Byrdon took her through the events leading up to Darla Lister's Death.

"Did you think she was going to kill you?" Jess asked her.

"Oh, she wanted me dead, alright," Juliette, answered calmly.

On her cross-examination, Linda Delgado leaned back against the Accuser's table, bracing herself with her hands. "Lady Juliette, how well did you know Darla Lister?" Her voice was suspiciously mild.

"I'm not sure I understand, Ma'am," Juliette responded.

"Come now," Delgado prodded, "if she did indeed try to kill you, she must have had a reason to want you dead, so I ask again, why she would want to kill you?"

Jess Byrdon stood up. "Your Honors," she protested, "please remind the Accuser she is dealing with a child."

After a quick glance at her two counterparts, the center judge brought a large crystal hammer down sharply on her bench. "Yes indeed, Dame Delgado, I caution you to moderate your tone when asking questions. We wouldn't want to frighten a little girl, now would we?"

"I apologize Your Honors," Delgado said smoothly. "I will restate the question. Lady Juliette, do you know why Darla Lister would want you dead?"

"Because I know too much about her, I guess," Juliette responded, stroking the dolls hair.

"What could a child like you possibly know that would make a grown woman want to kill you?" the Accuser rapped out.

"I know she was Thieves Guild," Juliette said flatly.

"Indeed? The Thieves Guild is reputed to be a myth," Delgado said condescendingly. "What makes you think it really exists?"

"Grouter, the man in charge of the placement center where I grew up was a Chieftain in the local Guild. Lister was his daughter and one of his sub-chiefs. I think she brokered weapons for him."

"Your Honors, this is ridiculous," Delgado protested. "The child is making up stories—"

"I am not!" Juliette cried. She pulled a data cube out from under her blouse and held it up in front of her. "Before we left, I stole this data cube from Grouter's office. It has all his files. Grouter was into a lot of stuff for the Guild, not just selling kids. This has all the information about his operations on it. He wanted it back and that's why he tried to kidnap us on Fenris."

Jess Byrdon looked stunned. Katherine and Zack exchanged glances. Delgado eyed the cube as if it were a poisonous reptile.

"Your Honors, I protest! If it's real, I should have been told about this before the trial started—" Delgado began.

Just then, a tall, grey-haired man in the uniform of the Interplanetary Patrol, who had been standing in the back watching the proceedings, came up the aisle. "Your Honors, if I may interrupt?" he asked.

The lead judge looked at him in exasperated resignation. "Why not?" she said. "We've got baby dragons and children testifying about myths in this courtroom, so what's one more thing, more or less. Please proceed, ah—what is your name?"

He bowed to the bench. "Double Nova Jefferies, Your Honors. With all respect to your Accuser, the Thieves Guild is not a myth. We've known about it for the past thirty years. For the past decade, Lady Juliette has been our informant in Grouter's establishment. Before leaving Fenris, Lady Juliette sent us a message letting us know she had evidence about the local operation on Fenris." He turned to Juliette, "I apologize for the delay Milady, it took some time for your information to reach the proper person and for me to arrange to come out here. May I have the cube?"

Juliette fumbled it, almost dropping it and then held it out to him, and he took it smiling. "Thank you. You are a very brave little girl. Your parents can be justifiably proud of you."

The judge looked at him. "You will inform us if there is any information about Darla Lister in there?"

"Oh, I can do better than that," he said, pocketing the cube and taking out another crystal. "This is a copy of one of Lady Juliette's reports from several years ago. It plainly shows Lister as being involved in

Grouter's operation."

He handed the crystal to the bailiff, stepping to the side with her as she verified the transfer of the information cube for the courts records.

"Well!" the judge looked for consensus at her two associates. "I think we have heard enough to make a decision, unless you have something further to offer Dame Delgado?"

"No, Ma'am, under the circumstances I guess not," the Accuser replied glumly, sitting back down at her table.

After a fast consult with her colleagues, the judge again brought her crystal hammer down on her bench. "It is the finding of this court, that Lady Katherine O'Teague had good cause to think her daughter, Lady Juliette was in mortal danger from Dame Darla Lister. Therefore, we find the death of Dame Lister to have been justified. Court is dismissed."

Double Nova Jefferies seemed to enjoy watching the jubilation at Katherine's release. Apparently in his position, he didn't often get to see an innocent person set free. When Juliette descended from the witness box, he bowed to her. "I wanted to thank you in person, Lady Juliette for your service to the Federated Worlds, and to tell you that if you ever need the services of the IPS, you have only to contact myself or my office."

"That is all very well, Double Nova," said Katherine coldly from behind him. "However, I question your wisdom in co-opting a child to spy for you."

He turned to her warily, recognizing the signs of a tigress in defense of her cubs. He knew the stance was real and not a pose because this woman just had been acquitted for killing another woman in defense of this girl. He coughed. "Milady, until I came here I wasn't aware of Lady Juliette's age. You see, although we have been receiving information from someone inside Grouters organization for several years, we hadn't identified her until the last message informing us she would be traveling with you." He looked down at Juliette. "It seems incredible..."

"It wasn't really me or me alone

until the last year," Juliette put in, glancing at him out of the corner of her eyes. "Before that, my friend Laylie got the information and taught me how to send the messages. She thought no one would suspect me, you see. Laylie worked for Grouter in his office. She was the one who taught me how to get into the data bases."

"What happened to Laylie?" asked Katherine.

Juliette gulped, and wiped her hand across her eyes. "I'm not sure. She disappeared from our rooms about a year ago. I think—well she was getting older, and Grouter—I think he was starting not to trust her."

Jefferies looked penetratingly at her. "Do you think he killed her?"

"Maybe. He might have sold her to Van Doyle though. Laylie was pretty and she was beginning to look more like a woman despite her disguises. Maybe you could find out?"

He nodded at her. "I promise you I will try."

Juliette looked up at him under her lashes. "Thank you."

Katherine studied her daughter thoughtfully. The behavior wasn't typical of Juliette. Juliette met her eyes deliberately for a long second before dropping her own.

"We will be holding a small celebration back at Glass Manor Double Nova," Genevieve said. "I would be happy to have you join us. If you haven't yet arranged a place to stay while on Vensoog, we would be delighted to have you as a guest."

"That is very kind of you, Laird O'Teague," he said in surprise. "Just now though, I need to get this information back to our local office so I can begin to make a record of it. I would be happy to join you later, if I may?"

Genevieve nodded graciously. "Of course. Any of the water taxis can give you a lift out to the manor. I'll let my people know to prepare a room for you."

She turned to her sister, "C'mon Sis, the children are hungry, and I think we need to get Jelli outside before she leaves any presents for the bailiff to clean up."

Upon his arrival at Glass Manor, Double Nova Jefferies was greeted with warmth and accepted into the family circle. After dinner Zack asked him for a private meeting.

When he reached the conference room, he found Gideon, Zack and Corporal Thompson, one of the former DeMedici soldiers who had accompanied Lister on the attack on Veiled Lodge, waiting for him.

"A group of Wilders helped us sneak onto Veiled Isle," Thompson stated. "And I know Lister was in contact with someone besides Lewiston, because she got several messages from whoever it was while we were in the hills just before we jumped the fishers. When we got a space drop with some extra weapons and supplies, Lakeer, the Wilder leader didn't seem too surprised to get it, and one of his gang mentioned it hadn't been the first time they had gotten supplies dropped that way."

"Yes," put in Zack, "and I suspect the crew that snuck in here the night before the trial started came from there as well. They certainly don't appear in any database we have access to, so they can't have come in with any of the new immigrants."

Jefferies regarded the men thoughtfully. "You've had them in custody for several days. Did you find out what they wanted?"

Gideon shook his head. "They wouldn't say, but after little Juliette's revelations this afternoon, I'm wondering if they weren't after the data cube. It must have some explosive information on it, for the

Guild to go to so much trouble to get it back."

Jefferies nodded. "I only had the chance to scan it briefly but it does. Some government officials and previously untouchables are going to be mighty unhappy very soon. They've made at least three tries for it. Your daughter must not have had it on her when Lister grabbed her and shoved her into that locker on the Dancing Gryphon," he told Zack. "I suppose Lister figured she might have a chance to search your quarters while everyone was looking for Lady Juliette. Or that it would stay lost if Lady Juliette were dead."

Jefferies stood up. "This has been a valuable meeting, Gentlemen. I assure you I will follow up on the information you've given me."

"If I might make a request, Double Nova," Gideon said. "All the clans have been troubled with raids from a Jack ship. Would it be possible for a Patrol ship to search the area for it? I think that would be in your best interest as well as ours. If they want what's on that cube desperately enough, your own transport might be attacked when you leave Vensoog."

Jefferies looked over at Gideon. "In the war, you gained quite a reputation as a strategist, Michaels. I can see it was deserved. I'll certainly put in a request for support."

The family stayed another three days at Glass Manor while Zack and Gideon attended meetings of the Security Council.

Chasing The Dragon

JEFFERIES had been gone for a day and a half when another representative from the Interplanetary Patrol arrived to take possession of Juliette's data cube. This man also used the name Double Nova Jefferies. He contacted Glass Manor from his ship in orbit, causing consternation because he claimed the other "Jefferies" had been a fake. He requested permission to prove his identity on arrival and was permitted by Gideon to come out to the Manor. When he appeared, his appearance was in marked contrast to his predecessor; he was short and thin with sharp black eyes.

Gideon, Zack and a security contingent met him at the docks when he arrived. He seemed unruffled at being disarmed when he landed.

"You said you could prove you are the real Patrol representative?" Zack asked.

"Certainly," he replied. "I realize that having been fooled before you won't accept anything I've brought with me, so I suggest you request verification from Patrol Headquarters. In the meantime though, there a way to speed things up if I can speak in person to Juliette Jones."

"Why do you want to speak to my

daughter?" Zack asked suspiciously.

"There are recognition signals she will recognize," Jefferies said, unperturbed.

"Yes, there are," said Juliette, who had come up quietly.

Zack interposed his body protectively between her and Jefferies. Juliette stepped around him and slipped her hand into his. "I understand you have some beautiful property on Sahara," she remarked, watching Jefferies.

He rubbed his nose with the middle finger and thumb of his left hand. "It isn't on Sahara," he said referring to one of the desert planets, "it's on the coast of Waterfall City on Aphrodite."

"One should never cast pearls before swine," she said agreeably, twirling a strand of hair around her fingers.

"Ah, but pearls of wisdom are always welcome," he replied, folding his fingers under his chin and bowing.

"He's okay," she said. "He has the right signals." She pulled a cube out of her pocket and held it out.

"I thought you gave that to the other Jefferies," exclaimed Zack.

"That one was the fake I prepared," she said. "I knew he wasn't my contact because he didn't have any of the recognition signals."

"And the story about your friend Laylie?" Gideon asked.

Juliette smiled, not really a nice smile. "That was Grouter's receptionist. I kind of hope the Guild does go looking for her. She was real mean to the kids; if you made her mad at you, she made sure you weren't fed, or she locked you up in a closet or something worse. I did have a friend who taught me about this stuff, but I saw him killed last year after Laylie turned him in to Grouter." Her voice was perfectly calm as was her expression.

Jefferies looked thoughtfully at her, "Grouter's staff disappeared when the Patrol raided the Placement Center. If you know where this Laylie might have run to, we might be able to turn her for information if we can find her."

Juliette shrugged. "He used the Grinders as foot soldiers, and some of them used their membership in the Grinders as steppingstones to move up in the Guild. She might have been one of them. Being Grouter's office drone was a lot easier job for a woman than earning your way on your back like most of the Grinder's girls did. Maybe she went back and she's hiding out with them."

Zack and Gideon exchanged glances. "Do you know if he's left the planet?" Gideon asked Jefferies.

Jefferies tapped his shoulder com. "Let me contact the local headquarters," he said. "This is Jefferies," he announced as the com crackled to life. "I need to check the status of a recent arrival."

"You don't sound like Jefferies," the voice on the other end said suspiciously.

Jefferies sighed. "Patrolman, check the ID on this communicator."

"I'm sorry, sir," the voice said meekly after a minute. "But he—Jefferies—I mean the other Jefferies had all the right credentials and everything."

"Never mind that now," Jefferies said impatiently. "I want to know if he's left the planet."

"Just a second." Over the communicator, there came noises of someone frantically moving objects and shuffling plastia sheets. "Um, no sir. I don't have a record of him leaving."

"What about the prisoners he took with him?" Gideon asked.

"What was that?" the voice asked.

Jefferies sighed and repeated the question.

"What prisoners?" the voice was

bewildered.

"Have any other ships or shuttles departed?" Zack asked.

This time the voice answered without Jefferies having to repeat the question. "There is a shuttle due to depart in about 10 minutes."

"Can you put a hold on it until we get there?" Jefferies asked.

"Uh—what reason can I give them?"

"Why don't you tell them you're getting readings showing a fuel leak?" Juliette, who had been listening quietly, suggested.

"But I don't have a fuel leak reading—"

"You aren't going to have to prove it, Patrolman," Jefferies snapped. "Just do it!"

In the meantime, Gideon had

called up any security forces he could find in the compound, and ordered them to report to the boat dock on the double.

Zack looked down at Juliette. "Go back to the house and wait with Katherine, Hon," he said.

"Yes," Gideon agreed. "Please let Genevieve and the others know what's happening, and that we'll be back as soon as we can."

"Alright," Juliette agreed.

On her way back, she contacted the other children and asked them to come to Violet's room for a private meeting.

The fake Jefferies and the prisoners were not on the shuttle.

Hostage

GENEVIEVE was hiding in her office, pretending to go over the Clan crop rotation schedules so she wouldn't have to admit her fear even to herself. It didn't help that she had begun to wake up feeling queasy every morning; today she'd had to pretend she was sending Gideon off to hunt trouble without being weepy about it. To distract herself, she had invited Jayla to join her so she could begin learning about the duties of a First Daughter, but the girl had pleaded a headache.

Gideon had left before dawn this morning to take an armed troop out to the Clans eastern boundary. A report had come in last night about a group of Wilders crossing into O'Teague lands from one of the smaller DeMedici isles. She knew it was ridiculous to be afraid Gideon couldn't handle a group of ill-disciplined Wilders without getting hurt, but a knot of fear sat in her stomach anyway. She understood enough now about her new husband to be aware that one of the reasons he generated such a fierce loyalty among his men was because he wasn't the type of commander who led from behind. Oh no, not Gideon. He got right down there in the mud and blood with them, she thought.

Not that she could have fallen in love with any other type of man. Oh Goddess, she thought, did I just admit I love him? Loving your husband wasn't such a tragedy, she comforted herself. At least it wouldn't be, she thought ruefully, if she could be sure he returned her feelings.

As it was, she couldn't be sure how deeply he cared about her, because he had never said the words. Except for that little item, he was almost perfect; he didn't flirt with other women, he was brave and kind-hearted, he was a considerate lover and passionate in bed. He could be trusted to support her decisions when he felt she was right and wasn't afraid to counter them if he thought she was wrong. But Genevieve wasn't sure how much of his behavior was because he was genuinely a good man with a well-developed sense of personal honor or because he truly was beginning to love her.

She was beginning to suspect her overly emotional reactions to questions like this and her queasiness in the mornings meant he had given her a child. He had admitted to her that he wanted a home and a family. I don't want a man who stays with me because of our child, she thought rebelliously. I want what Momma and Papa had.

She was staring unseeingly at the map of O'Teague crops in front of her when someone coughed to get her attention.

Mary, her assistant, stood nervously in the doorway clutching a sealed message. "What is it? Is Lord Gideon hurt?" Genevieve demanded.

"No, Milady," Mary said. "This

just came in. I was told to give it directly to you and not to let anyone see me do it."

"Well, give it here then. Do you know who sent it?"

Mary bit her lip. "Well, I can't be sure, but it came through the old way."

Genevieve was puzzled. "The old way? What old way?"

"Um, you remember when you and that Ivanov used to pass messages you didn't want your parents to see? I think it was the same man who gave this to me. He caught me as I was coming in from the kennels."

Genevieve looked at the missive as if it were a poisonous reptile. Slowly she broke the seal and read the message. Her blood turned to ice.

"Find Lord Lucas and my sister and send them to me. Then I want you to locate Lady Jayla and make sure she is still inside the castle," Genevieve ordered.

How could Gregor have managed to meet Jayla, she wondered, let alone see enough of her to develop the kind of relationship that she would consent to meet him in secret? Surely the child couldn't have been so foolish. But she had to have gone willingly to meet him; Gregor couldn't have taken her by force from inside the castle without raising a noisy riot, she reasoned.

Lucas and Drusilla arrived out of breath. "What is it?" Drusilla asked. "Mary was in a state when she told us to get here." Her Quirka chittered nervously on her shoulder and was answered sharply by Gorla.

Absently, Genevieve stroked Gorla's back. "Lucas, do you think you could reach Gideon today? You will have to go in person. I can't take the chance our communications have been compromised."

"Sure," he said. "If I take one the new air sleds, I could reach him in two hours. Are you calling him back? Because even if he took my sled, it would still be four hours before he got back, and the men don't have a sled that could keep up. They would be at least another two hours behind him."

Genevieve tapped the letter on her desk. "I hope it won't be necessary to recall the men he took with him," she was beginning, when

Mary burst back into the room.

"We can't find her," she said breathlessly. "George thought he saw her in the stables after lunch, and her mare is gone."

"Blast that child!" Genevieve exclaimed. "Here, you both had better read this," she said, handing the offending letter to Drusilla. "Lucas I'm going to have to send this letter with you to Gideon, and I need to write down what actions are going to be taken here as well."

Drusilla looked up from reading the letter and handed it off for Lucas to read. "You know I thought I saw Gregor in town while we were waiting for the ship to come in, but I didn't say anything because I didn't want to bring up bad memories. Besides, I was only about ten the last time I saw him. I couldn't be sure. Afterwards, I saw someone who looked like him out at the warehouses, but he was talking to Lewiston, so I just thought I had been mistaken. I'm sorry, Genevieve. Maybe if I had said something..."

"What could you have said?" Genevieve asked her, not looking up from the note she was writing. "The fact that two slime buckets were meeting wouldn't have meant much to anyone."

"I had Jayla with me that day," Drusilla remembered, stricken. "I left her in the shops while I made arrangements to load the cargo being brought down. Gregor must have met her then."

"Well, his pretty face always did

appeal to little girls," Genevieve said wryly. "Jayla would have been an easy mark too; she was unhappy and feeling left out of things. It would have been easy for him to play the sympathy card. But to take advantage of a child like that! I'm going to kill him when I find him."

"I doubt you'll have to," Lucas said. "If I know Gideon, your old buddy Gregor is a dead man. You aren't really planning to meet this guy, are you?"

"He says that's the only way to get Jayla back," pointed out Drusilla, "But not alone though, Sister. Even if he thinks he's gotten Gideon out of the way Gregor will have men with him."

"I agree," Genevieve said. "Furthermore, we can't be sure that the raiding Wilders aren't real, and I can't leave my people unprotected, so the men who went with Gideon will need to stay where they are. Drusilla how many security officers do we have here in Glass Castle right now?"

Drusilla was counting in the air. "About fifteen, I think."

"Alright, we have about six hours to kill, so I want you to quietly contact everyone you can, and arrange for them to meet you in the woods outside Miller's farm. Tell them to bring their camouflage gear, and full weapons. Gregor probably has someone watching the castle and I don't want him to realize how many fighters we'll be taking with us. Our people are to spend the next six hours getting in position to quietly take out Gregor's lookouts when you give the signal."

She signed the letter she had been writing, and folding the one from Gregor inside, handed it to Lucas. "Lucas, here is the letter and a map of where Drusilla and the men will be waiting."

"You're not sending Drusilla with the fighters!" exclaimed Lucas. "She could get hurt—"

"So can Genevieve," Drusilla interrupted him. "You have a lot to learn about the O'Teague women. We don't stand around and wring our hands while someone else fights our battles for us."

Genevieve ignored Lucas's objections. "Make sure Gideon gets the letter and the map, Lucas. I don't think Gregor will hurt Jayla while he's waiting for me to enter his trap, so I plan to wait at least four hours before I start out, and it will take me about a half hour in traveling time to get to the farm. If Gregor complains, I'll just blame his instructions to keep everyone from knowing I was leaving. Tell Gideon I'll do my best to stall Gregor until he arrives."

The transponder in the larger sled enabled Lucas to find Gideon and the O'Teague fighters hiding in a grove of trees just short of a mountain pass. They were waiting for the Wilders to come within reach of their ambush. Fearful for Drusilla, Lucas had pushed the Sled hard and arrived in under his two-hour time limit.

An annoyed Gideon frowned at

him. "What are you doing here? I told you to stay back at the castle."

"Genevieve sent me," Lucas said quietly. "She thinks this raid may be a diversionary tactic to get you out of Glass Castle. Here," he thrust Genevieve's message at him. "Read this."

"We got incoming boss," one of the men whispered to Gideon.

"Okay, proceed as planned," Gideon ordered. He stuck the letter and map inside his shirt to read later. "Draw a weapon from the sled and follow me," he ordered Lucas as he moved up to join his men.

The Wilders already had a few battered looking prisoners tied together with ropes and walking under guard. Gideon's snipers opened fire, taking out the renegades guarding the prisoners first and then as many others as they could. There was a short vicious battle before the remaining Wilders fled back into the mountain pass. As pre-planned, a group of O'Teague fighters separated from the main body and followed them.

Once he had made sure the captured Wilders had been secured and their prisoners released and given medical treatment, Gideon pulled out Genevieve's letter and read it. He swore ripely. "Do you know what this says?" he demanded of Lucas.

Lucas nodded. "I made up a little time on the way here, so you haven't really lost much, if you leave right away."

"Morton!" Gideon yelled. A tall,

black-haired man who was built like a bull came at his call.

"We've got an emergency back at the Castle," Gideon informed him. "I'm going to leave you in charge of clean up. Use your best judgement. Any prisoners will have to be taken back to the Castle for Genevieve's judgement. You'll have to send the wounded Clansmen back in the big sled. Lucas can pilot it, so you'll only need to send one man to bring it back. I'll get back to you as soon as I can. Any questions?"

"Nope, I got it boss. Good hunting and a safe landing." Morton said, using the soldier's traditional send off before a battle.

After Morton had returned to the rest of the men, Gideon and Lucas walked back towards where Lucas had left the sled.

"I'd like to beat her black and blue for taking this risk," he growled to Lucas, who had followed him.

"Jayla or Genevieve?" inquired Lucas.

"Dammit!" Gideon snarled. "The worst of it is I wouldn't lay a hand on either of them and they both know it. But I can dream about it."

Lucas laughed. "I understand. Do you know she sent Drusilla out with the fighters? They talked about murdering this guy Gregor for taking advantage of Jayla. I told Genevieve she probably wouldn't get the chance to kill that scum before you beat her to it," he remarked. "See you back at the Castle. Safe landing and Good hunting Gideon."

On the way back, Gideon made

better time than Lucas did if possible. His imagination kept giving him pictures of Genevieve captive in Gregor's hands. Knowing they had a prior romantic relationship until she discovered Gregor's earlier nasty plans to take over her clan made it ghastlier. He kept visualizing her beaten or raped, or what was worse from his point of view, being glad Gregor had kidnapped her.

It was getting dark when he found Drusilla and about twelve camouflaged fighters in the woods near the old farmhouse. "Bout time you got here," Drusilla said stepping out of the shadows.

Gorla jumped from a nearby tree onto Gideon's shoulder, chittering angrily into his ear and pulling his hair. "Okay, okay," he said stroking her back. "Relax, we'll get her back. How long has she been inside?"

"Only about ten minutes," Drusilla said. "Gregor has about ten guards outside as far as I can count, but there may be more inside the farmhouse. I've got people in position to start taking them out as soon as you got here." She touched the crystal at her throat and it briefly glowed red in the darkness.

Gideon started for the farmhouse. Drusilla touched his arm and said, "Wait until they're all down."

One by one, a single green flash lit up her crystal ten times. She touched it again and said quietly. "Okay, guards are down. Warlord is with us. Go in hot."

Drusilla took off, flitting from tree to tree so quickly she caught him by surprise. She might be young, but she obviously had been trained by experts. Briefly, he wondered if his foster son knew what he had fallen in love with. He set off after her.

Miller's farm had been a thriving operation before Wilders had killed the family. It was a sturdy dome house with several large outbuildings. The killings had taken place just as the war started and Genevieve hadn't yet found a family ready to move onto the property. A good place for a hideout, Genevieve thought as she rode up. She needed to get a tenant in here as soon as possible.

When she rode up one of Gregor's men tried to pull her off her horse, so she kicked him in the face and swung down herself. Ignoring the cursing man whose nose was dripping blood, she headed for the door. He shoved in after her, demanding to be allowed to teach her some manners.

"I told you not to mess with the merchandise," Gregor informed him. "It's your own fault. Go wash your face."

Genevieve knew as soon as she entered the farmhouse she wasn't going to have much trouble stalling Gregor. Gregor had three men with him who were standing around watching the show. When she was thrust into the room, she saw Jayla sitting at the table. The girl's hands were tied and the she appeared dull and lethargic. "Alright, I'm here,"

Genevieve announced. She moved towards the girl, intending to untie her, but Gregor blocked her.

"You said you'd let her go, if I came," Genevieve reminded him.

"I lied," he said. "But you knew that and you came anyway." He tried to kiss her on the cheek, and she jerked back.

"What happened to all that famous Ivanov charm? Why tie her up and drug her if she came to you so willingly?"

Gregor laughed, pleased with himself. "She was becoming tiresome," he admitted.

"So let her go," Genevieve said.

"Are you kidding? Kids this age are worth money, especially fresh ones. Van Doyle's looking to rebuild his stable since your sister managed to bust up his kiddie whorehouse on Fenris. Pretty little blond thing like her, he'll pay me big."

"You're a pig," Genevieve said in disgust. Jayla looked up at her, white-faced and silent, tears leaking down her cheeks.

"Oink, oink," Gregor said, "Anyway, she doesn't matter anymore since she got me you."

"You don't have me," Genevieve retorted. Her heart was wrung for the girl's stricken face, but it served her purpose to keep him talking.

"Oh, but I do," he responded. "I sent your new husband off on a wild goose chase, and I'll be sending him a letter from you saying we've eloped."

"Gideon won't believe you," Genevieve said. "By now he's

received a copy of the letter you sent me and is on his way here. If I were you, I would cut my losses and run before he kills you."

A flicker of what might have been fear showed in his eyes for an instant. He cast a sly look at the three watching Jacks who were clearly waiting to see his reaction. "You think I can't take out your big war hero?" Gregor sneered. "If he comes here he's walking into a trap. I've got enough men with me to grab him."

He grabbed her arm and tried to pull her to him. "Maybe, I'll let him watch when I take you."

Genevieve laughed in his face. "You tried to force me once before, remember? As I recall it didn't work out too well for you. You're pathetic,

Gregor," she said. "You're reduced to seducing schoolgirls now. What did you do, give the child a dose of Payome to make her compliant?"

He slapped her face, knocking her into the table. Genevieve recovered and kicked him in the knee. He tried to slap her again, but this time she ducked and he missed, losing his balance and falling into the table.

Gregor's men proved poor guards. They had stationed themselves around the walls so they could watch the show, and were blindsided when the farmhouse door burst open. Gideon, followed by Drusilla and three armed O'Teague fighters, rushed inside. Gorla leaped off Gideon's shoulder and dashed for Genevieve.

"Jayla, get on the floor!" Genevieve shouted, as pulsar fire erupted. Out of the corner of her eye, she saw Jayla ducking under the table. Two of the Jacks dived for the floor. The third took a pulsar hit right between his eyes and collapsed. The second Jack had managed to get off a shot and one of Drusilla's fighters went down, wounded in the leg. The other two O'Teague fighters went after the Jack with the Pulsar, each taking a different side of the room to reach him. Drusilla ducked a blow from the third Jack and returned a one-two punch to his gut before he managed to grab her.

Gideon had gone straight for Gregor and knocked him away from Genevieve. When Gregor's hand came loose from her arm, Genevieve fell backwards, landing hard on her rump and sliding into the wall. Gorla had clung to her despite the hard landing, and she cooed at Genevieve in concern, patting her face and snuffling at her hair.

Gideon wasn't having the fight all his own way however. Gregor had learned a lot dirty fighting techniques while with the Jacks. He rolled with his landing and came up drawing his pulsar pistol. Gideon saw it and kicked out quickly, knocking it out of his hand. Gideon tried to follow up the kick, but was knocked off balance and nearly fell when Drusilla and the third Jack careened into him as they grappled. Drusilla was skilled but she was losing; she was a tiny woman and the Jack was not only stronger than she was, but outweighed her by at least a hundred pounds. Eventually he would have overwhelmed her, but Toula, Drusilla's Quirka, jumped in to help her mistress. Her leap landed her on the Jack's head, clawing and biting at his face and ears. The Jack slapped at her, trying to sweep her off and got a fistfull of her poison-filled quills in his hands. His blows didn't succeed in loosening Toula's hold on him because she had her teeth too firmly buried in one of his ears. The pain from his torn ear and the blood running down his face into his eyes distracted him long enough for Drusilla to break free and kick him in the gut. He doubled over, and her next kick caught him under the chin. He stumbled into Gregor who had drawn his knife and was circling to reach Genevieve to use her as a hostage.

Gideon threw himself between Gregor and Genevieve, pulling his own knife from his boot. The two men closed with a clash of blades, cutting and slashing at each other.

Just then, Jayla who had been hiding under the table, spotted Gregor's fallen pistol. Her face a mask of fury and hurt, she picked it up and fired it at the two men.

"Jayla! No!" Genevieve cried. "You'll hit Gideon!"

Luckily the shot missed Gideon entirely hitting Gregor's knife hand. He screamed in pain, dropping the knife. Gideon forgot all his training and tossed his knife to Genevieve who caught it, and leaped on Gregor, furiously raining blow after blow on him with his bare hands.

In the meantime, the two O'Teague fighters had managed to disarm and capture the Jack with the pulsar. Drusilla threw the remaining Jack, who was bleeding profusely from his torn face and ears, over her hip and flipped him face down. Landing hard on his back, she secured his hands, already swelling from being stuck with Toula's quills, behind his back with plastic ties.

With immense satisfaction, Genevieve cuddled Gorla and watched her husband pound her ex-lover into a crumpled mess who lay gasping on the floor. When Gideon finally dropped him, one of the

O'Teague fighters moved in and knelt to put him in restraints.

Stepping forward, Gideon delicately removed Gregor's pistol from Jayla's shaking hands, put it on safety, and stuck it into his belt behind his back. He held out a hand to Genevieve and Jayla and pulled them both up off the floor into his arms for a fierce hug.

Staring dispassionately at the sobbing heap on the floor, Drusilla remarked, "I think Gregor was waiting for contact from a ship in orbit."

"Yes," agreed Mia, one of the fighters who had followed Drusilla and Gideon into the farmhouse. "While we were waiting for Lord Gideon to get here I overhead two of the men talking about it. This idiot thought that if he had our Laird, he could take over O'Teague. He planned to use us as a base to attack the other clans."

"Any of the men with him still alive?" inquired Gideon turning back to look at Gregor.

"Two besides him and these two," Drusilla said. "What do you want to do with them?"

Gideon had been watching Genevieve comfort a weeping Jayla. Now he looked over at Drusilla. "We need to find out more about this Jack ship. They obviously want something, and I'm betting it isn't just food or trade goods. If it's just a single outlaw ship, it needs to be taken out so it can't raid us again. But I don't think this is a solitary raid; there's too much support being given for this to be a lone Jack ship. I think more is going on here. Haul the wounded down to the jail in town. Vernal used to be pretty good at interrogation. We'll ask him to come over from Veiled Lodge to question them. I want to find out who is really in control of the Jack ship, what their plans are and if Lewiston was involved in this little stunt."

"What about him?" Drusilla asked, pointing at Gregor.

Gideon shrugged. "Ask your sister. I understand the Laird passes judgement on lawbreakers. Besides, since he's from another clan there might be some political ramifications."

Genevieve had been instructing one of the O'Teague fighters to take

Jayla to the infirmary. "Make sure
Elsie checks her out for Payome,"
she said. "I think that animal dosed
her with it."

"Yes ma'am," the woman said,
putting her arm around Jayla's
shoulders and leading her out.

"Genevieve?" asked Drusilla.

"I suppose there will be political
consequences. Blast it, we just went
through this over Katherine killing
that bitch Lister," Genevieve said.
"The Tsarina took Gregor back after
her mother kicked him out years
ago for raiding, so I suppose we
need to go through diplomatic
channels before judgement is
passed. I'm afraid we're going to
have to suffer through another
Council trial. The usual sentence for
kidnapping, extortion and collusion

to commit murder is execution."

"You'll still need to contact the Tsarina," Drusilla reminded her. "Maybe she will give permission for us to try him here on O'Teague. It would certainly be less embarrassing for her."

Genevieve made a face at her. "Why don't I delegate that to you? I'm tired." She sat down with a thump in one of the empty chairs.

"Yes, I agree you need to do more delegating and I can certainly make the initial contact, but I don't think you can hand over this one," Drusilla stated. "In your condition though, you need to start getting more rest and the best way to do that is—"

"Her condition? What condition?" Gideon interrupted in alarm.

"You haven't told him?" Drusilla asked.

"When did I have time? Besides I haven't had the test to confirm it yet."

"What condition?" Gideon yelled. "If someone doesn't start answering me—"

"I missed my time of the month," Genevieve said.

"Your what?"

"You know," Drusilla said, "that thing that happens to women every month? Bleeding, cramps, irritability?"

Genevieve waited while he assimilated the information.

He started adding things up and a big grin broke over his face. "You're going to have a baby?"

"Well, I haven't had the test yet,

but I think I might be. Hi Daddy," she added.

When they returned to Glass Castle, Gideon practically dragged Genevieve into the infirmary despite her protests that she was fine, only tired. She was informed that a drowsy Jayla had already been treated for the overdose of Payome and was half-asleep in one of the infirmary beds.

"How did you know about the Payome?" Doctor Else demanded waving the results at Genevieve.

Genevieve hesitated. "Gregor has a history of using it on women, not necessarily to enhance sexual performance but because in higher doses it makes a person lethargic and easier to control. How much did he give her?"

Else made a face. "Well fortunately, not enough to cause a dangerous overdose, but I'd like to keep her here under observation for tonight."

Genevieve nodded. "Good. If you're finished with me I'm going to go to bed and sleep for about two days."

"That's a good idea," Elsie said. "Come back tomorrow and we'll start you on a nutrition regime. Need to keep that baby healthy, you know."

Planetary Politics

WHEN GENEVIEVE went to infirmary the next morning to check on the Jayla, she found her sulking because the medic hadn't released her.

"I brought you some clean clothes," Genevieve said, laying them on the end of the girl's bed.

It was plain that Jayla was in a foul mood. "Did you come here to gloat?" she asked Genevieve resentfully.

"Gloat?" Genevieve repeated. "About what?"

"He wanted you, not me," was the angry reply. However,

Genevieve heard the tears under the snippy tone.

"Who? Gregor? Gregor never wanted a woman in his life except to bed her. What's more when he did, he could care less how the woman felt about it," Genevieve snorted. "Gregor always did say whatever it took to get him what he wanted."

Jayla frowned at her. "He made me think he was my boyfriend, and then when I went to meet him, he said he was going to sell me. Then when you got there he said I was a child and he wanted you instead," her voice was doubtful.

"Oh, I'm sure he said all of those things," Genevieve replied, "but Jayla honey, he didn't say he wanted me because he loved me. He said that because he thought raping me would humiliate me. That's why he wanted me. When he was done, he would have sold me to those slavers too."

For the first time since she had come into the room, Jayla looked Genevieve full in the face. "I thought—" she began. "I guess I've been a fool, haven't I?"

Genevieve sat down on the chair next to the bed. "Oh, honey," she sighed. "We've all been fools for love one time or another. It's the nature of humans. If it makes you feel better, I was four years older than you are now when he fooled me. Don't be ashamed of loving the man you thought he was. I doubt you will ever misjudge a man's character so badly again."

"How do you know?" the girl

asked curiously.

"Because now you know what a liar looks and sounds like. And if you're ever in doubt, just measure the new man against your Uncle Gideon or your Uncle Zack or Uncle Vernal. You see, a real man will care more about the happiness and safety of those he loves than he does for his own interests. A man like your uncle does that for people in his care or under his command whether he loves them or not because it's his duty."

Jayla cocked her head to one side and regarded Genevieve oddly. "You say that as if you don't know if he loves you or not."

Genevieve nodded seriously. "Well, I don't know for sure, because he hasn't said he does.

What I do know is that even if he doesn't love me, I can trust him to put the well-being our people over his own because that's the kind of guy he is. I hope you can appreciate that."

"I'll try," Jayla said humbly.

"There's something else you should know. There may be a public trial about this. I'm going to have our lawyer do her best to keep you from having to testify, but you need to be prepared in case that happens. The lawyer will come out here to talk to you about that and about anything else Gregor might have told you concerning his plans. Are you going to be okay with that?"

Jayla bit her lip, but nodded. "Yes. I can do it."

"Good girl."

Genevieve's next step was to contact Jess Braydon, who agreed to file the complaint against Gregor for attempting to kidnap Genevieve.

"I know Katherine's daughter stood up well enough on the stand, but having it come out about the way he used her will be really humiliating for Jayla," Genevieve said. "I want to avoid that if I can."

"I think we should leave the girl out of the complaint for now," Jess agreed. "If we play it right, we can use his treatment of her as leverage to make the Tsarina agree to our terms."

Genevieve nodded. "I plan to contact her after this. I'll let you know the outcome."

"I'll be in the office the rest of the day preparing the complaint," Jess replied. "Contact me at your convenience."

Just as Genevieve was about to open her communicator, Gideon came in and closed the door.

"I thought you might need me in case she wants another witness," he said.

Tsarina Veronika was visibly upset by what Genevieve had to tell her. "You have a history with my brother," she said suspiciously. "How do I know this isn't about getting back at him for making a fool of you all those years ago?"

Genevieve hung on to her temper. "Look Veronika," she said quietly, "This isn't about the past. Gregor ceased to be important to me a long time ago. Are you seriously going to tell me you haven't made the connection between his return to Vensoog and the sudden influx of Jack raids? Because you would have to be a fool not to be suspicious and one thing I am sure of is that you most certainly are not a fool."

"I don't want to believe it," Veronika Ivanov declared. "He's my brother, dammit. How old did you say this girl is?"

"She is thirteen," Genevieve replied. "I can furnish you with the medic's lab report on what was found in her system if you want it. We have the two captured Jacks from the ship doing the raiding and several witnesses, including Warlord Gideon."

Veronika was silent a moment, then she blew out a deep breath.

"This is going to cause a major stink, O'Teague. While not everyone was happy with my decision to bring Gregor back, he worked very hard to gain supporters when he returned. Perhaps you had better send along a copy of the medics report and depositions from the witnesses," she said at last. "Gregor made himself very well-liked so the reports will make things—easier, when I inform the Grand Council about this."

"Does that mean Ivanov Clan isn't going to contest the charges?" Genevieve asked.

Veronika sighed. "I need to read the report myself. If it supports your story, I can pledge that the Clan won't mount a defense, but that won't prevent Gregor or some of his supporters from doing so. Whatever you may have heard, Ivanov isn't a dictatorship. Clan members do have rights."

"I do understand," Genevieve said. "I just hope you understand that there is no way this can be hidden the way it was before. I believe, and so does most of my security force, that the Thieves Guild is behind the raids and that they have a deeper agenda than just gathering money and produce to sell for high prices to planets impoverished by the war. We think they may have plans to set up a permanent base here on Vensoog. Given Gregor's history with them, we can't just let him be shipped off planet like last time. However, if he tells the Security Council everything he knows, O'Teague will support taking execution for his crimes off the table."

"Thank you," Veronika said quietly.

"Get things ready," she told Jess Braydon later. "I'm forwarding a copy of the medical report to the Tsarina as well as summaries of the witness depositions."

She saw the imminent protest on her lawyers face and said quickly, "It's the only way to ensure Tsarina Veronika won't mount a Clan defense for him, Jess, and you know it."

Jess made a face. "I suppose. Just you make sure you only send her the bare minimum, though. I don't want that nasty piece of slime having time to think up excuses."

Genevieve gave her a mock

salute and signed off.

Rumors of War

IT HAD BEEN a month since Gregor's attempted kidnapping of Genevieve and Jayla, and there was a lot to be done before his trial in Port Recovery, which had been set for after the Planting Season to ensure all the Clans could attend. Genevieve looked up from the documents displayed on the screen on the top of her desk when Drusilla knocked on the open door of her office. "Since when do you knock when you want to talk?" she asked.

"Is this a good time? I know you still have a lot to handle after the storms and with the trial coming up, but I just got a com from Katherine.

I'm going to need to be over on Veiled Isle for a few weeks because Mistress Leona apparently slipped and fell going down the stairs to the wharf. She broke her ankle and Cora says it will be several weeks before she can walk on it again. Apparently, she's been teaching Katherine's daughter Violet at home because Katherine refused to let her go to the Talker's Guild for training. Katherine told me she would get in touch with you about me spending some time on Veiled Isle," Drusilla added.

Genevieve nodded, "She did. Wasn't Mistress Leona one of your teachers?"

"Yes. She came over from Talkers Isle at Mothers request because I was so young when my talent manifested."

Genevieve looked thoughtfully at her baby sister. Under the neutral tone of Drusilla's voice, she sensed faint disapproval. She folded her hands over the screen and nodded. "Yes, Katherine told me about her decision to have Violet tutored at home. Look, I know you and Katherine have always disagreed about sending young children there for training. You need to remember that your experiences there were very different. For you it was good thing, for Katherine it wasn't".

Drusilla made a rude noise. "That's because of that friend of hers who killed herself during training. There is more than one side to that story, you know."

Genevieve smiled placatingly at

her. "That's what I mean. For the sake of family harmony, please don't try to convince Katherine to send the child away. Other than that, I don't have a problem with you being gone for a few weeks. You have been a Goddess gift the past few months when I had to be gone so much. You did such a great job in my absence, that I've gotten spoiled. I certainly think you're due some time to handle your own duties."

Drusilla looked at her curiously. "Are you going to train Jayla to be a First?"

"I'm considering it," Genevieve admitted. "Do you think she can handle the job?"

"Maybe," Drusilla answered. "She sure did a bang-up job during the

Swarm/Storm. I guess we'll have to see. Does she want it?"

"That's a good question," Genevieve said wryly. "One I haven't asked her yet. On another matter, do you want to travel with us when Gideon and I go out the Isle at the end of the week? We planned to stop there when we take that group of security trainees out to Talkers Isle. Mary can handle things here for the few days I'll be gone."

"I'd like that," Drusilla said. "It will be nice to have a few days of family time; it's been a long time since we were all three together for any length of time. Katherine wants me to temporarily take over Violets training, and to find another Talker to help out Mistress Leona after she recovers from her fall."

She hesitated and then asked, "Is Lucas going with the new trainees?"

"Yes, he is," Genevieve replied. "I've been meaning to ask you if his attentions are becoming a problem."

Drusilla made a face. "Truthfully, I don't know. I mean, I do like him, but I think he's interested in more than just friendship and I don't know what I feel about that."

Genevieve opened her mouth to reply, and then shut it again. "Baby Sister," she said finally, "I know you had some bad experiences as a child when you were overwhelmed with other people's thoughts and feelings. You know now that you were too young and inexperienced to know how to shield yourself. I just wish you would stop using that as a reason not to trust your feelings now. Why don't you give it a try?"

The day after Katherine and her family returned to Veiled Isle, Rupert set off on a cross-valley trip with his mentor and several others to gather wild plants. The plants were to be dried and processed into the medicines, perfumes and other toiletry items to be traded and sold by O'Teague merchants to the other clans, or exported off world as a luxury product.

"He needs to learn to recognize the plants grown in the wild as well as those we cultivate," explained his mentor Jora to Katherine who was fretting because they still hadn't caught all the Wilders who had invaded during Roundup.

"Milady, you know we always go

out to cull the plants this time of year," Jora said.

Zack exchanged a look with Katherine. "If a security detail goes with you Jora, it should be safe enough," Zack told her. "However, I insist that the detail be fully armed. There still might be Wilders in the uplands."

"Very well," Katherine agreed reluctantly. "Who are you planning to assign to the security detail?"

"The six who scouted with me during roundup," he replied.

Katherine frowned. "You do realize that Lucinda is being mentored by Loren, and Loren was a part of that team? That means Lucinda will be going too. We will have two children out there—"

"Katherine," Corrine said softly,

patting her hand, "children learn best by doing the job they are training for. This will be a part of Lucinda's life in Security. Loren is a competent and able security mentor. She will make sure Lucinda takes no unnecessary risks."

By the time Genevieve and Gideon arrived on Veiled Isle at the end of the week Rupert and Lucinda had been gone for ten days and Katherine's worries had been somewhat eased because there hand been no Wilder sightings.

Because they were escorting the twenty security trainees destined to take Talker training, Genevieve and Gideon had used one of the larger air transports rather than catching a ride on a slower Fisher ship headed for the waters off Veiled Isle.

When Genevieve and Drusilla visited Mistress Leona, they found that lady glaring morosely at her bandaged foot, which was propped up on a padded stool.

Drusilla immediately gave her a hug, asking, "How are you feeling?"

"Like an old fool," replied Leona crossly. "The damn steps were wet or I wouldn't have slipped. You need to get down to the beach as soon as possible and check to make sure all the nests have been cleared of ticks. There will be a new crop of Sandie calves born soon after the dragons come out of hibernation, and we don't want more of them dying...and Jelli will be waking up soon. Violet was in here this morning worrying about it."

"I'll check the beaches before we

leave for Talker's Isle," Drusilla promised. "I'm going to see about bringing you back an assistant to help with your duties. This post was supposed to be a comfortable place for you to retire. We never intended for you to need to set up new classes."

"That's a good idea," Katherine said as she joined them. "Because I think her class size is going to be increased. I just got a message back that Rupert and Lucinda found an orphaned nest of Dactyl kits. Apparently, the mother was shot and barely made it back to the nest before dying. They haven't been weaned yet and are being bottle fed by Lucinda and Rupert."

"Have they bonded to them?" Leona demanded.

Katherine shrugged. "It seems likely."

She touched Genevieve's arm, "Sister could I see you outside for a few minutes?"

When Genevieve followed her out the door, Katherine shut it. "They found a wounded messenger in the dome shelter when they arrived. She claims to be from Doña Gracile DeMedici, with an urgent message for you."

"Gracile, isn't that Sabina's younger sister?" Genevieve asked. "I wonder. You know I couldn't get through to LaDoña when I tried to discuss the situation of those six soldiers who surrendered to Zack. It's beginning to look as if something smoky is going on in DeMedici. Wounded did you say?

How?"

"I don't know for sure," Katherine admitted. "Zack borrowed your airsled as soon as he heard and went to see for himself. He's pulling the gathering crew out of there and leaving a bigger security detail to search for intruders." She bit her lip. "To tell you the truth, I will be just as glad to get my children home if there's raiding going on."

Genevieve looked at her shrewdly. "You don't fool me Sister; you're worried about Zack too. Gideon went with him, didn't he?"

Katherine nodded slowly.

Genevieve made a face and touched her belly, which was beginning to develop a small bump, protectively.

"You don't seem surprised Gideon

went too. Does he jump in feet first a lot?"

"You could say that. If his men are in trouble, you can bet Gideon will be right in it with them. He's a good leader Katherine. I think Zack is too and they won't take any unnecessary risks."

She patted her belly again. "Well, we can't change who our men are so I suppose we'll just have to wait and see what this messenger says," she said briskly.

"When are you due?" asked Katherine having noticed her earlier gesture.

"In about three months," Genevieve admitted. "We haven't announced it yet, but I took the test and had it confirmed. I wanted to inform close family first."

"Congratulations!" Katherine gave her a big hug. "Does Drusilla know?"

"Of course. She was the first to spot it," Genevieve said wryly.

"How are you and Gideon getting along?" Katherine asked.

Genevieve looked startled. "Fine. Why do you ask?"

"Well, Zack and I have decided we want to make our marriage permanent. We plan to hold the Forever And A Day commitment ceremony during the Festival. I was kind of hoping we could make it a double."

"Katherine, that's wonderful! I'm so happy for you," Genevieve said giving her sister a hug. "As for Gideon and myself, well, sometimes I think he might go for it, but he's never said anything."

Katherine refused to be put off. "How do you feel about it, sister?"

"Yes, I want it," Genevieve admitted a little crossly. "Your matching program worked great, okay?"

Katherine's eyebrows rose. "So, what's stopping you from asking him?"

Genevieve glared at her. "I'm the Laird and I'm carrying his child. What if he says yes because he thinks he has to?"

Katherine looked thoughtful. "He doesn't seem like that kind. But I suppose you could lead into it by just asking him what he wants to do when the year is up. He gives me the impression of being a man who would say what he wants when the opportunity to do so is offered. If he wants the commitment to last, I think he'll tell you so. Why don't I arrange a picnic on the beach for just the two of you; that will allow you some uninterrupted time alone."

"Alright," Genevieve agreed. "But let's hear what this messenger has to say first."

The Messenger

ZACK AND Gideon arrived back at the lodge the next day with the gathering crew and the injured messenger in tow. The messenger's arrival took a back seat with the assembled clan to Rupert and Lucinda's arrival with the baby Dactyls. Dactyls were rarely found outside the wild and everyone wanted to see them.

"Oh, aren't they just the sweetest things?" Juliette cried. The Dactyl kits were smaller than a Quirka and covered with soft, plush fur in a mottled red, which fluctuated under all the attention. They had large pricked ears and a pointed nose on a small foxlike face. Their bright eyes viewed the crowd with caution. Their short hind legs were equipped with tiny sharp talons, fur-covered wings folded against their sides and they had stunted arms with front paws resembling hands. Lucinda and Rupert immediately handed off one of the pair each carried to Roderick and Juliette.

"They're hungry," Lucinda informed Juliette. "Feeding will go much easier if each of us takes one."

"What do they eat?" Juliette inquired.

Drusilla took charge. "Dactyls are hunters whose diet consists mostly of meat although they do eat some vegetable matter," she explained. "These look as if they're still nursing, so we need to fix up a milk formula and some bottles."

She looked thoughtfully at Lucinda and Rupert. "Have they bonded to you yet?"

Rupert hesitated. "Well, this one seems to always look to me to feed him, is that what you mean?"

She nodded, turning to Lucinda. "And you?"

Lucinda snuggled the kit, stroking its tiny head. "Well, this one seems to like me the most. I just thought it was because she seems to be female."

Drusilla held out her hands. "Let's see."

When she lifted the kit from Lucinda, it let out a shrill wail and continued to whine while she held it.

"Stop that, silly," Drusilla

admonished. "I'm not going to hurt you." She turned the kit over and examined its rear and belly. "Yes, this is a girl." She handed it back to Lucinda, and the kit quieted immediately.

She smiled at both children. "Well, judging from that behavior, I think it's safe to say the pair of you will be joining Violet in my Talker's class, next week."

"What about us?" asked Juliette, stroking the back of the kit she was holding.

"Yes, I suppose you had better attend," Drusilla said. "The chances are good that those two will bond to you and Roderick if you feed and handle them a lot."

"Here," Violet thrust four small filled bottles at the others. "While you talked, I went down to the kitchens and fixed these up for you. I hope the Milk formula is about the same as Jelli used."

"Thank you, Violet," Drusilla said. "We'll have to check with the husbandry chief to make sure the formula is correct, but I expect you are probably right. Well, get started kids. You've got hungry pets to feed."

Jelli stuck her nose up to the nursing kits, sniffing interestedly. She shook her head and let out a loud sneeze. The kits ignored her.

"I think Jelli was hoping they'd be Sandies," Violet said.

"She won't hurt them, will she?" asked Lucinda protectively.

"Of course not!" Violet answered indignantly." "She knows they aren't food."

Drusilla chuckled. "I doubt the kits are in any danger from Jelli," she said reassuringly. "Come on Violet, let's go and visit the Husbandry chief and get some bedding prepared for the new family pets."

As soon as Cora would let them in, Gideon and Genevieve were joined by Katherine, Zack, Vernal and Corrine in the Messengers hospital room.

"She's very tired," they were told. "But she wants to talk to you as soon as possible, so I'm allowing it. However, if she starts showing signs of stress, I'm going to kick you out."

As soon as the messenger saw Genevieve, she grabbed her hand.

"Please, you've got to help us!" she whispered.

"Help you with what?" Genevieve asked.

Tears leaked out of the messenger's eyes. "He's a devil," she wept. "Doña Gracile knows he's giving Doña Sabina something to make her obey him. LaDoña knows too, but she can't do anything. He just came in and dismissed all her regular servants and guards before we knew what was happening. She's surrounded by his men now. She isn't even allowed to answer the com or speak to anyone unless he okays it."

Genevieve patted her hand. "You are safe here, my dear," she said. "But I do need to know what is going on. Exactly what kind of help do you want?"

"It's all in there," the messenger said, handing Genevieve the leather pouch she had been clinging to.

"Alright," Genevieve said, taking the pouch and extracting the crystal and plastia sheets. "Dr. Cora says you need to rest. I'll read through this, and I will come back and talk to you tomorrow. In the meantime, try and get some sleep."

Once they had all read the letter from Doña Gracile, they were stunned.

"Goddess," Katherine uttered, after Vernal set down the letter. "How did DeMedici let this happen?"

"They trusted him because Doña Sabina vouched for him," Zack pointed out. "The way you vouched for us."

"They had warning," Genevieve reminded him. "I gave LaDoña a copy of the recording Katherine transmitted."

"Lewiston's a pretty slick character," Gideon said, "and we do know that he was giving Doña Sabina Submit to control her. I'm not that familiar with how it works. Does anyone know how long the effects last?"

"About forty-eight hours," Juliette volunteered. As First Daughter, she was privy to the discussion.

Vernal looked thoughtfully at her. "How do you know that?"

She stroked the back of the sleeping Dactyl kit that was snuggled up against her shoulder. "I saw the effects first hand a couple of times on some kids Van Doyle returned as 'unsatisfactory'. They had been knocked around quite a bit. Some of them didn't make it."

Katherine put a comforting arm around her shoulders. "I really hope someone kills that man in prison," she declared.

"Got to put him there first," Zack reminded her. "As far as Lewiston taking over, it wouldn't be that hard. His crew were armed, and they probably outnumbered the standing security force. No offense, Genevieve, but our unit could have done something similar to O'Teague if we moved fast enough after we landed."

"Thank you," she retorted smartly.

Gideon coughed. "Yes, well that wasn't why we came to Vensoog. I think we have to assume that most of Lewiston's men weren't in on the scheme either—just his command crew. Otherwise there would be too much chance of someone talking out of turn."

"I suppose," Corrine remarked sadly. "However, we need to decide what answer to give this messenger to take back with her."

Genevieve looked startled. "You don't think I should formally present this request for help to the clan?"

"Of course," Corrine smiled, "after we decide what we want to do so we can convince them it's the proper action."

"Well," Genevieve said, "we can't afford a full-scale war just now. We don't have the security forces to spare or the funds in the treasury to maintain such an action."

"We might send supplies as a humanitarian gesture," Katherine proposed.

"Yes," Corrine added. "And there is that stockpile of old weapons and ammunition your grandfather hid in the caves behind Horned Cove. I suppose we could give them a few of those."

"What kind of weapons, and are they in working order?" Gideon asked.

"How many?" Zack added his question before she could answer.

"Let's go take a look," Vernal suggested.

"Fine, you three do that," Genevieve agreed. "Corrine, you remember how to get into the caves don't you?"

"It's been a while," she answered, "but I think I can find it. Why?"

"Because Drusilla and I need to take those trainees over to Talkers Isle," Genevieve reminded them. "We need to do both things as soon as we can. I don't like leaving Jayla to handle things with only Mary to help her. She's too young and she hasn't been trained."

"Are you going to name her as your First?" Katherine asked curiously.

"Nothing has been decided yet," Genevieve replied. "She really handled herself well during the storms, but she still doesn't fully understand what the job would entail. Once she does, she may not want it."

Talker's Isle

THE TALKERS Guild was technically independent from the Clans, who each sent potential Talkers to the Guild for training. Upon completion of training, a Talker was given the option of becoming a member of the Guild. If they chose to become a member, they had to take an oath vowing allegiance to the principles of the Guild over any loyalty to their clan. However, anyone could take the training and then return to their former occupation, which was what Gideon and Genevieve planned for their security trainees.

Talkers Isle was a small island with tiny subsistence farms and almost no industry, off the southern coast of Veiled Isle. It had no seaport to speak of either, just a few shallow coves, so visitors usually traveled to it via airsled. It wasn't officially under the jurisdiction of the O'Teague clan, but since it lay within the clan's boundaries, the Planetary Council had declared O'Teague accountable for its defense. O'Teague usually found itself responsible for supplying the Guild with most of the food and other staples needed, but the other clans also brought in foods and clothing.

Unknown to Genevieve, the night before everyone went their separate ways, Gideon took Lucas and Tim Morgan aside.

"I need both of you to keep your

eyes and ears open for potential problems while you're there," he said. "Gregor and Lewiston both had help from somewhere in this area. Talkers Isle is independent of Genevieve's control, so it would be a good place to set up a fifth column."

He handed them both small communication crystals.

Morgan looked doubtfully at the tiny crystals.

Gideon laughed. "I had them made this small so they could be hidden easily. They are a lot more powerful than they look. If you see or hear anything suspicious, give Zack a call and he can contact me. Don't get yourselves killed, either," he added dryly.

Morgan snorted and indicated he was headed for bed. When Lucas would have followed him, Gideon put out a hand to stop him.

"Is something the matter?" Lucas asked him.

"No, nothing's wrong, but we need to talk. Why don't you sit down," Gideon suggested. "This might take a while."

Lucas sat, looking at his foster father curiously.

"How much do you know about your family?" Gideon asked him.

Lucas gave him a puzzled look. "Why I know who they were—I mean what my parents and grandparents names were. I know we originally came from Wales and somewhere way back we're related to one of the Bards. In fact, Taid's official title was the Bard of Lewellyn. Why?"

Gideon took a crystal on a silver chain out of his pocket and handed it to Lucas.

"What's this?" the young man asked.

"Your grandfather wanted you to have that when you became a man," Gideon responded. "He left it up to me to know when to give it to you."

Lucas held the chain up and looked into the crystal. "Is it some kind of message crystal?"

"Not exactly," Gideon said. "From what Owen told me, you don't put it into a machine to read it. You hold it in both hands, open your third eye and it will speak to you. Until you feel ready, you are supposed to wear it with the crystal against your skin."

"Why give it to me now?" Lucas

asked.

"Let's just say I think you're ready or you will be very soon and let it go at that, okay?"

"Okay, I guess." Lucas slipped the pendant chain over his head and tucked the stone inside his shirt.

Forever And A Day

GENEVIEVE and Drusilla returned from Talkers Isle with the Mid-Level Talker Drusilla had chosen to assist Mistress Leona in tutoring the children. In Genevieve's opinion, Dame Joanne was a sour faced woman with an equally sour disposition. However, she had been eager to accept the position, and she was the only volunteer.

"I can't force anyone to accept the job," Drusilla had protested when Genevieve expressed her opinion of Dame Joanne. "She has her reasons for wanting to leave and

Mother Superior expressly requested I consider her. I will be on the Isle to monitor her interaction with the children," Drusilla reminded Genevieve.

"I trust you did explain to Dame Joanne that Katherine is very protective of her children?" Genevieve asked.

"It will be fine, Sister," Drusilla said firmly.

"So, when are you and Gideon going on your picnic?" Drusilla asked, changing the subject.

"When he gets back from inspecting those weapons I suppose," Genevieve said and then added in exasperation, "Does everyone in this family know my private business?"

Drusilla laughed at her. "Of

course, we do. That's why we're family."

Genevieve wasn't present when Mistress Leona met Dame Joanne, but she heard about it from Katherine.

"The estrogen output in that room was awful," Katherine said, chuckling. "Once they get over who is assisting who, though, I think it will be alright. At least Drusilla has promised to stay and make sure none of the children get caught in the crossfire if the two of them really lock heads."

Since all three of the men had felt leaving the weapons in the Horned Cove Caves would make them too easy to steal once word of them got out, the weapons had been removed from there and brought back to be placed into a storage room down in Hidden Lake Cavern. This was explained to the women in some detail at the family conference the night the men returned with the weapons.

"The weapons couldn't be left there because once you hold a clan meeting about handing over some of them to the DeMedici rebels everyone will know where they are, including the Wilders and the other clans" Gideon patiently explained.

"And you think this is better?" Corrine snorted.

"Well, it certainly will make them a lot less reachable by any Wilders," Vernal told her.

"By putting a big fat target on the Lodge."

"It doesn't have to do that,"

Katherine said slowly. "The Clan Charter only requires that we inform the Clan executive council about decisions that might have a negative impact on the clan. It doesn't say anything about informing the Clan at large. Four of us on the Council are sitting right here and we have a majority vote. Our cousins are still too young serve, so we only have to convince their guardians to agree and keep quiet about where we're storing them."

"Who do you have to tell where the rest of the weapons are going to be stored?" Juliette asked.

Everyone looked at Genevieve for an answer. "What our Clan Charter requires us to tell the Council is a pretty broad mandate," she said thoughtfully. "In fact, if we make giving Gracile a few of the weapons a onetime thing it probably won't be noticed. I don't think there will be any objections as to our simply giving Doña Gracile's refugees food as a purely humanitarian gesture. That is easily defended if Lewiston happens to complain to the Security Council."

"I agree," all three of them said together.

The day before Genevieve and Gideon returned to Glass Isle dawned bright and sunny. If Gideon was surprised at Genevieve's suggestion that the two of them take advantage of the day and picnic on the shores of the underground lake he didn't say so. The crystals in the cave walls gave off a pale blue light providing visibility and giving the entire area the ambiance of a fairy world. As it was a weekday, the recreation area used by the Katherine's people located halfway around the shore of the lake from the mostly empty animal enclosures, was unoccupied this afternoon.

"This is beautiful," Gideon exclaimed, kneeling to examine the blue sand at the edge of the water. "The water is so clear. Are there fish?"

When Genevieve didn't answer him, he turned around to find she was facing one of the naturally occurring alcoves with her hands on her hips.

Someone had gone to the trouble of setting up a table and chairs inside the alcove. To the left a blanket sized, soft white pad had been stretched out. Gideon set the picnic basket down.

"Did you do all this?" he asked.

"Sorry, the basket of food was as far as I got," Genevieve said resignedly. "I think I know who we thank for this though: Drusilla."

He eyed her "You don't sound entirely happy. It's a beautiful, thoughtful gesture."

Genevieve sighed. "Oh, I know, but—sometimes I get tired of everyone in the family knowing our business!"

He laughed at her. "Well, we can thank her later, he said equably. "C'mon, strip and let's go swimming."

The lake water was warm and peaceful. Insensibly, Genevieve found herself relaxing. When they finally came out of the water, she put on the Dragon Nest silk wrap Drusilla had laid out for her. Looking down at herself, she realized ruefully that her tummy was protruding. As she sank down in a chair, she accepted the glass of fizzy water Gideon poured for her. He had left the wine bottle unopened.

"You don't have to forgo the wine just because I need to you know," she said.

He shrugged. "It's not a hardship."

Genevieve had dithered on how to ask the question she wanted an answer to all the time he had been gone inspecting weapons. She had finally decided to just ask it.

She took a deep breath. "Katherine told me that at the

Planting Festival, she and Zack are going to change their commitment from A Year And A Day to Forever And A Day. She wanted to know if we would like to make it a double ceremony."

When she looked up to meet his eyes, she found him watching her intently. "What did you tell her," he asked.

"I told her I would ask you," She said, "I don't want to put pressure on you if you don't feel comfortable with the idea—"

She broke off with a gasp. Gideon had stood up and pulled her out of her chair, kissing her until she was limp and boneless against him.

"Does that answer your question?" he demanded.

"Well, sort of," Genevieve said

breathlessly, "but the words would be nice too."

"They would," he agreed. "Suppose we say them together?"

She threw her arms around his neck. "Yes!"

"I love you,' they said together.

A Historical Note

WHEN opened for colonization, the Founders had considered themselves fortunate that Vensoog was a semi-tropical paradise. Strings of islands of various sizes connected by channels of water (although of a slightly higher saline content than oceans on Old Earth) were strung around the equator between five larger landmasses. Two ice-covered regions were found at each of the magnetic poles.

Every year the Islands and the five semi-continents were subject to swarms of insects that pollinated the entire planet. The double moons in a close orbit created heavy tide surges during the storm season that followed the swarms and cleared out the insect population. Abundant mammalian and avian life populated the planet; a variety of edible fish lived in the sea. The planet boasted several species of mammals the settlers dubbed Nessies and Sandies or Water/Sand Dragons because of their resemblance to the fabled mythical beasts of old earth. Some of the native species were found to be empathic with chameleon abilities; the Water/Sand Dragons, and a small vermin predator the settlers dubbed Quirkas. There were several varieties of furred mammalian flyers bearing a resemblance the Old Earth Legends of the Pterodactyls, who shared the empathic and chameleon characteristics of the Sandies and Quirkas. Because the Quirkas were small, cute, and soon seen to be able to bond with humans, they were quickly adopted as pets. They proved adept at hunting the varieties of small vermin and insects that tended to infest homes and animal enclosures. The smaller varieties of Dactyls were sometimes adopted as household pets, but the larger breeds who preyed on the Water and Sand Dragons proved difficult to domesticate.

The temperate climate of the islands proved hospitable to both man and the variety of animals the settlers brought with them to suit their agrarian lifestyle. A spaceport was developed on an island, expediently located next to the largest continent. Unfortunately, the settlers had copied other spaceport designs without taking into consideration Vensoog's weather. The high winds generated by the first storms toppled the Space tower and the settlers were forced to rebuild, wisely adopting a dome architecture style for the remaining buildings. The new colonists chose to settle first on the Islands closest to the spaceport for convenient access to the supplies being brought in, and had just begun to spread out onto the larger islands and explore the major continents when the Karamine Wars which had been going on an intermittent basis for years, broke out again and reached Vensoog.

The society the colonists created

had been one of the social
experiments designed on Old Earth
after the last planetary war. Space
exploration had become cheap with
the discovery of an efficient faster
than light drive. It had become easy
to colonize a planet where a group
could carry on with its sociological
theories undisturbed by conflicting
viewpoints. In those days, all it had
taken to develop a colony was
enough money to register their
claim to the planet with the
Confederated Worlds and buy ships
and supplies to launch out into
space with like-minded colonists.
The founding colonists that settled
on Vensoog had been led by a cadre
of wealthy women who decided the
male-controlled society governing
most of the Old Earth was the cause

of most of the wars that continually afflicted it. Recognizing that struggles for power had produced most of the strife in the past, the colonists theorized that changing the way in which political power was handled would change how society reacted to resolving conflict. The colonists blamed the breakdown of the extended family on a lack of responsibility felt by both men and women for the children they created. To counter-act these influences, they designed a planetary government loosely based on clan structures copied from Old Earth with a ruling parliamentary body made up of representatives from each clan with provision for additional seats to be created as the need occurred. Inheritance of titles, ruling offices and property would descend through female lines instead of the male. Recognizing the need for planetary cooperation, representatives from each clan met several times a year to make major decisions concerning planetary welfare. This body regulated laws in areas outside of immediate clan control, such as River and Ocean navigation or joint Clan ventures. Since the clans all came from different ethnic groups and ancestry on Old Earth, they each had different ideas of how they wanted their clan to be run. It was agreed that inside their own jurisdiction, each clan was free to set up different sets of laws to reflect their ancestral traditions, providing those laws adhered to the principles set down by the colony designers.

The discovery of valuable deposits of Azorite crystal power stones on Vensoog became highly prized as an export and made possible many of the non-mechanical solutions to the difficulties facing the new colony.

While the group of "wise use" ecologists who colonized Vensoog had preferred non-technical or non/industrial solutions to planetary problems, they were not averse to using gene manipulation to achieve the "non-mechanical" effects they wanted. Often, they genetically enhanced abilities already found in the domestic animals and plants they brought with them from Old Earth.

The Clan based culture was

supposed to provide a stopgap when individuals fell through the cracks of society. The founders reasoned there would be less violence if everyone felt they had a place in the social order, and the loose makeup of a clan would provide room for individuals who wanted to improve their lot in life or move up the social scale. It had been determined that a factor causing trouble in the past was the power holders (males) wanted to ensure their families kept what had been earned, but they had no real way of guaranteeing it was their own descendants who inherited since they could not be sure if their progeny really belonged to them. A woman on the other hand would always know to whom she gave birth.

Vensoog was not a true matriarchy (men were allowed hold positions of power, but could not pass along those positions or property except through their daughters). Allowance was made for those individuals who for one reason or another simply didn't want to join a clan; they fell under the authority of the clan's joint Security Council.

To ensure their plan for establishing a society was not tampered with, rigorous psychological testing had been given to the original prospective colonists to certify they would be flexible enough to adapt to the new power structure. Additionally during the voyage, the new colonists were subjected to sleep training and mental manipulation to accustom them to accept the changes. After two hundred years on the planet, the social order was firmly enough established so that the mental manipulation during sleep fell into disuse.

Unknown to the prospective colonists, they had been tested for "special talents" and high aptitudes with psychic gifts. The overt reason for this was allegedly that greater empathy should encourage group consensus. The covert reason for selection was that several of the clan bloodlines had always had the talent to perform what could have been termed "magic" by uninformed persons.

The founders had miscued on several assumptions. The theory that greater empathy would provide group consensus had not proven out. While inbreeding had produced high levels of certain types of psychic ability, it had not improved either communication or willingness to heal areas of disagreement. Human women were just as susceptible to jealousy, envy and downright cussedness as were human men.

The Karamine wars (Stardate circa 2626—3840) between the Confederated Worlds of which Vensoog was a member, and another star-faring race humans had come into conflict with, wreaked havoc on both sides. It left some planets in radioactive ruins and others devastated by Biologenitic weapons. Economic disaster, starvation and anarchy now stared many planets in the face. After nearly fifteen years of sustained warfare, the humans and their allies finally managed to piece together a truce of sorts. In truth, the truce had come about because both sides had used up resources to such an extent that they could barely feed their populations and maintain communication within their sphere of influence. In the Confederated Planets, outlying planets like Vensoog now fought off onslaughts from pirates who preyed on them using captured ships, and subsisted on meager alliances with the few Free Traders who had managed to hold aloof from the conflict.

The Karaminetes usual policy was to burn off a planet opposing them unless it had strategic importance or resources they could use. On planets that they deemed too valuable to destroy, they used biogenetic weapons When the Karaminetes noticed the large deposits of the valuable mineral Azorite that Vensoog had in abundance they had attacked it with a devastating bio virus. On planets they didn't burn off, the Karaminetes practice was to use conquered native populations as slaves. A study of human societies had convinced the Karamine Legion that in human society the males were traditionally the most rebellious so the Bio-weapon used on Vensoog targeted males. As a result, all the men and boys on the planet who didn't die outright from the virus were rendered sterile. The virus had no effect on the female reproductive system since the Karamines planned on harvesting ova from captured females and creating more women slaves, expecting them to be more tractable.

Happily, the virus had a very short life span and dissipated after a few months, which would have allowed the Karaminetes to settle on Vensoog themselves in time.

Fortunately for the colonists, the truce was declared before the Karaminetes took possession of the planet. Although no more attacks would be coming, the colony was still in deep trouble. The reserves of viable sperm from the lower mammals brought along for colonization in the freezers at the original landing site had been protected from the weapon and periodically replenished by the colonists. Unfortunately, in the two hundred years after making landing, the Vensoog colonists had used up all the frozen human eggs and sperm they had brought with them to ensure the colony remained biologically diverse. With no new children being born, the colony faced extinction. The planet's population would die out within three generations, unless something could be done to re-introduce new viable human sperm to allow more children to be born. Each of the clans worked frantically to come up with a solution.

After studying the political and physical mess left by the war, Lady Katherine O'Teague had come up with a plan to restore biological diversity among Vensoog's human population. She concluded that the best candidates for new colonists would probably be found among returning soldiers. While Vensoog wasn't the only planet to suffer from the bio-bomb virus, many other planets not deemed worthy for Karamine resettlement had simply been burned off leaving thousands homeless. In theory, the Confederated Worlds military force was composed equally of men and women, however, the majority who chose a career as soldiers were still male, and the men whose worlds had been destroyed were going to need new homes.

The Clans agreed to present proposals adopting the displaced soldiers on the planets in their sector of space who would be receiving many the refugees. Vensoog would accept new immigrants providing anyone who applied could pass the immigration screening and was willing to either take part in a temporary Handfasting agreement with suitable Vensoog women or provide genetic material. Clan representatives traveled to Fenris, Camelot, and Avalon where many of the returning soldiers were going to be decommissioned. After the first wave of ex-soldiers had been assimilated on Vensoog, the clans had agreed the screening program would remain in place on Fenris and the other planets for other potential new immigrants to use. A joint clan undertaking with Vensoog volunteers from each clan willing to take up temporary residence on these planets would have to be found to administer the screening programs.

Gail's Other Books

SPACE COLONY JOURNALS

Options of Survival

Destiny Rising

Tomorrow's Legacy

The Interstellar Jewel Heist

The Designer People

Alien Trails

Secrets of the Stars (ETA* Fall 2020)

PORTAL WORLD TALES

ST. ANTONI SERIES

Warriors of St. Antoni

The Enforcers (ETA* Spring 2020)

MAGI SERIES

Spell Of The Magi

Magi Storm

NON-FICTION

The Complete Modern Artist's
Handbook

PAMPHLETS

Introduction To The Internet #1

The Hard Stuff – Handbook #2

Art Show Basics – Handbook #3

Framing on a Budget – Handbook

#4

Are You Making Money? – Handbook

#5

*ETA is subject to change

About The Author

GAIL DALEY is a self-taught artist and writer with a background in business. An omnivorous reader, she was inspired by her son, also a writer, to finish some of the incomplete novels she had begun over the years. She is heavily involved in local art groups and fills her time reading, writing, painting in acrylics, and spending time with her husband of 40 plus years. Currently her family is owned by two cats, a mischievous kitten called Mab (after the fairy queen of air and darkness) and a Gray Princess named Moonstone. In the past, the family shared their home with many dogs, cats and a Guinea Pig, all of whom have passed over the rainbow bridge. A recent bout with breast cancer has slowed her down a little, but she continues to write and paint.

Author's Note

This book was previously published under the title Forever And A Day as book 2 in the Handfasting Series. It had a few sales, but it wasn't selling as well as the quality of the book merited. After consultation I was told that the title read like a romance book which was off-putting to science fiction readers (the genre it belongs in).

I have re-titled both the books and the series to better fit in the Science Fiction genre.

Thank you for reading this book. Reviews are bread and butter to independents like me, so it would be much appreciated if you could write a review and share it on the site where this book was purchased.

If you would like to know when my next books are coming out, please follow me on social media sites or sign up to receive E-mail notices

http://www.gaildaleysfineart.com/contact-us.php

E-mail lists are never shared with 3rd parties under any circumstances, and you will only receive notices about my books.

Excerpt: Tomorrows Legacy

SOMETHING was wrong on Talkers Isle. Drusilla had known it almost as soon as she stepped off the shuttle yesterday. This Isle had always been one of her favorite places on Vensoog. It's aura of peace and tranquility had provided solace to her angst-ridden spirit when she first set foot on it as a child. Now, someone or some*thing*, had poisoned that aura and Drusilla was going to make them pay for it.

The acute contrast between the atmosphere today and the feeling when she came here years ago as a traumatized child had been just nasty. When she had come as a child, it had been for further training in controlling the impact of the emotions she picked up from the people around her.

Today when Drusilla had come back to Talker's Isle to bring some of the clan's security forces here to take the Dragon Talker training, she had looked forward to immersing herself into the Isle's peaceful aura for a few days. Apparently, that wasn't going to happen.

"Alright," Genevieve said, her voice jerking Drusilla out of her brown study. "Enough brooding. Are you going to tell me what's wrong?"

"Can't you feel it?" Drusilla questioned. "This whole place *reeks* of despair, dissatisfaction and anger."

"I'm not a Dragon Talker," her sister reminded her.

"Trust me, something is very wrong here."

"Have you discussed this bad feeling with Mother Superior?" Genevieve asked.

Drusilla shook her head. "I don't think she's well, Genevieve. I don't want to distress her. I know something is not right though. When I asked for a volunteer to go out to Veiled Isle, it was almost as if the Talkers were hostile to the idea. When I was training here, teachers used to trip over each other to volunteer for a sweet assignment like that."

Her sister made a face. "Well I

don't think that sour-mouthed old bat who volunteered will be an asset. Why on earth did you choose her?"

"She was the only one to come forward, Genevieve," Drusilla reminded her. "I can't force anyone to come out to the Isle, you know that."

"So, what are you going to do?" Genevieve inquired. She and Gideon were expecting their first child during the Planting Festival, and Drusilla had noticed she had developed a habit of patting her belly protectively. She did it now.

"Someone needs to find out what is going on, but I can't stay here and root it out. I promised Katherine I would go back to Veiled Isle and help with tutoring Violet and some of the other children while Mistress Leona is laid up. I think I need to talk to Lucas," Drusilla said thoughtfully. "He's going to be here for at least eight weeks and he is a trained investigator. Once we know what is wrong, we can decide what steps to take."

"That sounds like a good idea," Genevieve remarked, reflecting with hidden amusement that over the past year Drusilla seemed to have developed a lot of confidence in Lucas. I do hope he's on her List because I think they might make a good match after all, she thought. I'll have to ask Katherine to check when we go back to Veiled Isle.

Drusilla had met Lucas, who was here to take the training, the first day he had arrived on Vensoog with

Genevieve's husband Gideon. Lucas was Gideon's foster son and he had emigrated with him when Gideon married Genevieve. Gideon's marriage to Genevieve, as well as that of many of Gideon's unit who had chosen to take part in the Handfasting, had been necessary to restore a healthy genetic balance to Vensoog.

Although Drusilla and Lucas had been considered too young to participate, the two of them had spent a lot of time together. Lucas had been the first young man to pay her the kind of attention a man gives an attractive woman, and Drusilla had found herself immediately attracted to Lucas as well. His quirky sense of humor and sturdy common sense had appealed to her. He wasn't bad looking either. Lucas was tall, with a born rider's broad shouldered, narrow hipped build, but his body showed the promise of the heavy muscles that would come as he aged. Like his foster father Gideon, he had light hair that he kept short soldier fashion, sharp green eyes and clean cut features.

To Drusilla's bewilderment and secret delight, Lucas had seemed to be charmed by her person and had spent as much of his time with her as he could manage. Lucas hadn't been annoying but he had made it obvious he wanted her. She sensed he wasn't going to be patient with her waffling about deciding forever.

For the past several months he had shown all the signs of a man who wanted more than just friendship, and Drusilla knew she was going to have to decide about her relationship with Lucas soon because the Makers were going to give them their Match Lists at the next Planting Festival.

Behind them, she could hear Genevieve's two foster daughters, Ceridwen and Bronwen playing with a new litter of Quirka pups. Drusilla's own Quirka, Toula, nuzzled her ear gently in sympathy with her unease. Quirka were native to Vensoog. They were about the size of a human fist, with thick, mottled yellow fur that changed color to match their environment. Originally making their homes in the trees and living on nuts, berries and insects, Quirkas had become avid hunters of the pests and creepy-crawlies who invaded human dwellings. Their main protection against predators was their retractable, venom tipped quills running down the backbone. They had a large bushy tail used for ballast when leaping from tree to tree. One of their chief attractions to humans though was the life bond they developed with certain men and women.

Leaving Genevieve and the children playing with the Quirka pups, she headed for the student dormitory area. Drusilla spotted Lucas's tall form in one of the dormitory sections kept for temporary training classes. Tomorrow, she knew the incoming class would begin the rigorous conditioning designed to give them the mental and physical stamina needed to turn them into Dragon Talkers. Tonight however they were given free time to settle in.

When she appeared in the doorway, Lucas immediately came toward her. "I need to speak to you," she said softly, "Outside."

This caused some good-natured teasing as he ushered her outside.

"Sorry about that," he said smiling. "Most of them know I've got a special feeling for you. They don't mean anything by it."

She waved it away. "Look, there's something funny going on here on the Isle. I can't stay and root it out, but since you have to be here anyway, I thought maybe you could look around some."

If he was disappointed at her

reason for seeking him out, it didn't show in his face. "Sure," he said, putting an arm around her shoulders and giving her a one-armed hug. "I'll keep an eye on things for you, but I want a real date when we get to the Festival."

Drusilla almost stamped her foot in exasperation. "Honestly, is that all you can think about? I tell you there might be trouble brewing and you want to talk about our Match Lists?"

"Well, what is going on here on the Isle is important, but then I think we are too."

"Oh, alright!" she exclaimed. "We can go to the Introductory Ball together, okay?"

"You got it Darling," he said, managing to plant a quick kiss on her mouth before walking away. "Oh, by the way" he said over his shoulder, "I was going to keep an eye on things anyway; Gideon already gave me a watching brief on it."

This time she did stamp her foot. How did he always manage to knock her off balance? No one else did that to her because she didn't allow it. Somehow though, Lucas always managed it

. Despite her irritation at falling for his trick, she watched him walk all the way back to the dormitory, unwillingly admiring the effortless way he moved. She couldn't help but appreciate his cleverness, despite her irritation because he had tricked her again. Somehow, Lucas roused a response in her physically and emotionally in a way she had never allowed another man to do, and darn it, he *had* managed to kiss her again. Drusilla sighed in exasperation. The problem wasn't with Lucas, she admitted. If she hadn't kissed him back every time, he wouldn't have reason to think she was falling in love with him. The real trouble, Drusilla acknowledged, was she was afraid he was right. She wasn't exactly proud of her behavior; it wasn't fair of her to allow him to kiss her and then push him away. It wasn't Lucas's fault she was afraid of the emotion growing between them—she knew was leery of her own power and what a loss of control could mean to others around her.

Irritably, she kicked a pebble off

the path back to the guest quarters. She had looked forward to the peace and tranquility she had always found here, but she hadn't found it on this trip. Yes, someone was going to pay for spoiling Talker's Isle. Drusilla intended to make sure of it.

CPSIA information can be obtained
at www.ICGtesting.com
Printed in the USA
BVHW031721041119
562865BV00001B/2/P